# BRIMSTONE

JUSTINE ROSENBERG

Published 2019

Printed in the United States of America
Print ISBN: 978-1-951490-07-2

Publisher Information:
DartFrog Books
4697 Main Street
Manchester Center, VT 05255

www.DartFrogBooks.com

*For Jamey.*

At midnight in October, Ava came home to a broken door. It stood ajar, gaping around the cold and dark. A piece of deadbolt thudded onto the seafoam carpet. No sound emanated from the little flat. She let herself in, just as the murmur of voices and the drag of boots boiled up from the landing below.

Her tin rings clicked against the revolver tucked into her coat. The noise was of knights crowding into the atrium, but they were not here to chase off thieves. This building was full of crooks. It was a khat raid, perhaps, or an ivorywoman whose long run had come to an end. Ava took off her shoes and pushed the door shut. She crept through the foyer, palms damp against the weapon's grip.

Everything was as she had left it. Only the paneled window stood out of place, thrust into a tangle of fog. Weak moonlight glittered upon the face of the Climbing Sea, and blue night birds cooed in the eaves, their warbles piling like dust into corners and cracks.

"Hey," she said. Her breath hung in the freezing air. "I have a gun! There are knights downstairs, you hear me?"

When no answer came, Ava repeated herself, first in Khardsog, then in halting French. Her knee clipped the edge of the claw foot table. It was a drunk, perhaps, filled with blue smoke and brandy from the Paper Houses. She stopped, revolver lifted against the shadows that webbed the bedroom and its musty water closet.

Behind her, something stirred. She pivoted when an empty champagne bottle plunged from the counter and burst against the floor.

"Wait," said the intruder. He spoke with slow precision, in a voice that slid like sand down her spine. "I did not take anything. It was an accident, coming here."

Blood roared under her skin. His eyes were pinpricks of red. Ava squared her shoulders, fingers tightening around the revolver. "You're a wraith." The hairs on her nape prickled and rose. "Those knights are looking for you, aren't they?"

He said nothing in reply. She raised one hand to show him that it was empty. "I'm going to turn on the light," she said. "We can't see in the dark like you."

His nod was a scarlet gleam. She kept the business end of her weapon trained on him, although she knew it was useless—no aether on the bullets—and tugged at the overhead chain. The bare lamp sputtered and choked. Her burgundy skirts shone, waterlogged from sloshing through smog-soaked alleys. She set her jaw and stood as straight as she could beneath her thick green coat.

The wraith crouched, naked in the recess flanked by a marble counter and an ebony desk. Her eyes followed the spare lines of his body. Curiosity threaded her fear. In the evenings, she saw them at market, for sale to brimstone mines and brothels in the west. Standing this close to one felt strange, as if the fabric of the city had come loose at its edge.

"Don't move," she snapped. "If I scream, the knights will be here faster than you can breathe." In the drawing room, the clock chimed a brassy note. The revolver wavered in her hands.

He was smaller than the others, wiry muscles coiled beneath a dark expanse of skin. There were twigs in his hair, and leaves wedged between the horns that curved away from his skull. He nursed a pair of bloodied knuckles. The bowstring curve of his mouth quivered; the flesh between his legs lay heavy and quiescent. He smelled of sweat and snow, and something barbed that she could not place.

"Please." His words dripped with fear. "I am not here to steal from you, and I must not be caught. What the Emperor does to us is wrong. You know this."

"I'm not the Emperor," she said, flatly.

Outside, voices flooded the hall. There was a rap on the door beside hers. "Open up, in the name of His Holiness, Emanuel Tong!"

Ava cringed. "That's Captain Shaw," she said. "Tell me, quickly! Where were they freighting you to?"

"The Americas," he said, sullenly. "To a fighting ring. I was sold yesterday night."

Ava set the revolver down with a thump. Her limbs turned to stone. Captain Shaw would accuse her of whatever he could. She still recalled the first time that her flat had been robbed, no less than an hour after settling the last chair in its nook. He had come when summoned, stepping over her upended bookshelf and broken china cabinet.

"I see no signs of an intruder, Ms. Sandrino," he said. "It seems that your workmen were clumsy."

The fine for filing a false report arrived in the

mail one week later. If Captain Shaw could not prove that Ava had stolen the wraith, he would see her in prison for harboring fugitives.

Next door, the neighbor said goodnight and turned his lock. Muted footfalls filled the hall.

"The bedroom," Ava said, clawing the revolver into a drawer under the sink. "You can hide in there. Keep still, and don't make a sound until I tell you it's safe."

A loud salvo of knocks made them jump. The wraith's red eyes darted between the window and the foyer. Then he whirled, scrambling for the unlit space like a hare into thorns. Ava shut him in and turned the handle.

"Tong Family business," Captain Shaw boomed.

"Self-important prick," Ava muttered, shedding her jacket as she marched for the door. When she yanked it open, light poured over the fractured tiles. She put on an absent grin and peered up at the armored man. "Good evening, Captain," she said. "How can I help you?"

Ezra Shaw was all teeth in the lamplight, wearing a smile so broad that it squeezed the mirth from itself. His dark hair was neatly bound, and the lines of his jacket were sharp over the blocky tell of a bulletproof vest. The dove and anchor glowed chrome-bright along both celadon sleeves. "Ms. Sandrino," he drawled, resting a gloved hand against the lintel. "Just got in?"

"It's been a long night, Ezra," said Ava, grin wilting. "I'm tired. What do you want?"

"Wraith got loose." His gold signet was pressed with the hoop of the imperial moon. Its wide band beat steadily against the plaster wall. "It escaped from a slipstream leaving Selang. The beast is making a run for the Northern Dark." His fingers stopped drumming. "These creatures," he said. "They like stray women and bad air. Just thought I would ask."

"Stray women," she repeated. His eyes grazed her breasts, and the thought of how he might look after her tea kettle met his face flitted across her mind. "You mean whores." Ava leered. "Why don't you say it? You shouldn't be afraid of the word. I'm certainly not."

"Now, Ava." Captain Shaw grew clumsy with ire. Ava saw the old fault lines open again: the vein that creased his brow, his shoulders drawn taut as wool on a shuttle. "The Knighthood holds all its citizens in the same regard, and you know it."

"Well, you are bothering one of your citizens, Ezra Shaw." Ava stood on her toes so that her forehead reached his chin. "This isn't the Americas. I keep a ledger of clients. I pay taxes.

Paper House business is legal—*and you know it.*"

"You were always such a spiny girl." The smile returned, unctuous and white. "Keep your ledger if it suits you, and throw your halfpennies at the House of Tong." He glanced at the scarred wood of the doorframe. "The Empire has prospered enough to let you be. North of Thrace, your sisters are culled by firing squads. They say it's kept the scarring sickness at an all-time low. Just remember that."

"I will, Captain," Ava replied. "Just you remember me while you're stretching your little stipend to keep your new wife in silks. Or are you back in your dad's pocket again?" Her laughter felt like ice. "The old man must be crazy for her. Dacian, right? A good Sambrese name. Orchid Coast girls like me are no good for marriage, just charity and fucking."

The lintel creaked under the Captain's hand. His face paled. He glanced over his shoulder, leaned close enough for her to smell the dark eddies of his perfume, and snarled, "You watch your dirty mouth when you talk to me, Ava Sandrino. You're speaking to a knight."

"I was a knight too, until the proctors caught you rubbing yourself between my tits." She folded her arms. "How embarrassing. Celibacy is hard to abide by. Lucky your father is well-connected, and lucky for me, I quite took to my new job." Behind her, the clock chimed again. "It pays well," she said, "despite what you imagine. I enjoy my fancy wines and trips to the coast almost as much as you enjoy rations and floggings. There's nothing to see here, Ezra. I'll make sure to send for you if the wraith tries to stiff me."

Face scorched, Ezra withdrew his hand. "Goodnight, Ms. Sandrino," he said, after a few seconds of open-mouthed fury. "See to it that you do. You don't want to be selling your services in a Tong prison. They make you give it away for free." He spun on his heel, whistling for his knights as he stomped up the hall.

Ava slammed the door. She put her shoulder against the splintered plywood, waiting until the ring of metal dimmed and the fire escape beside the northern landing opened and shut. Then, she crossed the kitchen floor on shaking legs and rattled her bedroom lock. "Hey, wraith! You can come out now."

The handle turned. He stood at the foot of her narrow bed, fingers resting on the frets of her blackwood mandolin. Crystal tumblers glowed between straining bookends; the teeth of snowbell incense split the night.

"You lied." His face was slack with disbelief. "I did not think you would."

"Ezra says you're searching for the Northern Dark," said Ava, sharp with fear. "People come out of there. Only geomancers go back."

"That is not true." The wraith cradled a blood-caked hand against his stomach. "I have spoken to those who have glimpsed it. It is special. A space between worlds." For a moment, he looked as if he wished to tell her a secret. "I will leave now," he said.

The cold collected in her bones. Ava rubbed her eye, smearing kohl across her cheek and fist. The last thing that she needed was for word to spread about a wraith leaving her flat. She held the bedroom door open and stood aside. "New Dera is crawling with knights. You can go after four. Sleep on the loveseat tonight."

He blinked, uncomprehending. "The red chair," she said. "There's a blanket on the coffee table. Don't try anything smart," she added. "You're nothing but missing cargo to them."

"I would not hurt you." The hard line of his shoulders drooped. "You have been kind."

"Kind." Ava scoffed. Wraiths were draft horses. The House of Tong forbade them from making or buying clothes, in case anyone forgot. They were impervious to cold, bringing up three times their weight in brimstone beneath the bite of the whip. They did not know kindness, and they certainly did not dream of waterways beyond the Northern Dark.

"They look miserable," she had whispered to Ezra, almost a decade ago. They'd stood together in the freezing belly of the barracks, filling their tins with coffee under the watchful eye of a commander in white.

"Who?" Ezra scowled.

"The shipyard wraiths. The ones for Babel."

"Oh, Ava." His hair was flecked with light from an oily stove. "How can they be miserable? They have no idea where they are or where they're going."

There was nothing that Captain Shaw did not know. The remnants of his certainty, solid and clean, set her nerves on fire.

"Help yourself to whatever is in the kitchen," she told the wraith, before remembering that they did not eat or drink.

He stepped towards her, palms out. Ava felt the breath leave her lungs. His smell was copper and earth, radiating out on a wave of inhuman heat. A crooked smile pulled at the corners of his mouth. She imagined running her thumb along the bend of his swollen lip.

"I am Sariel," he said. "You are Ava." He held out a hand, and looked immeasurably pleased when she took it. His grip closed around her fingers like a vise. "Thank you. I will not forget."

"Don't," she said, freeing herself delicately from his grasp.

She shut the door after him, waiting in silence under the eye of an antique clock. When five minutes had passed, she heard the muffled clink of forks and spoons. Dimly, she realized that the revolver lay in an unlocked drawer, but it was the thought of her flatware, rearranged under his curious gaze, that made her heart sink.

Flakes of moonlight drifted through the mulberry curtains. Ava went to draw a bath, leaving her clothes in a pile on the floor.

\* \* \*

In the close darkness of the water closet, she counted her earnings, running her fingers over the worn bills until she was certain that her sums were correct. Most of it was locked into a safe that clung to the basalt sink. The rest she hid between the saucer and pot of a pink-tipped cactus. A new coat was in order, perhaps, or socks that kept out the rain.

By the window, a pair of dancing shoes spun on yellowed laces. Lopsided shelves lined the wall. Old calling cards—dry cleaning, khat vendors, a paper square pressed with the head of an ibis—fluttered back and forth across the pitted wood, jostling for space with costume jewelry and thrift store songbooks. Ava had stacks of melodies piled away into chests and trunks: flights of notes from valleys in the far west, teahouse ballads, rhymes that she had written and scribbled out, never to glance at again.

She filled the brass washtub and sank beneath its curlicues of steam. A pleasant ache throbbed in her legs. The Paper Houses were busy tonight. Its patrons did not want dances or songs, or beguilement by trick coins and fortunes. This was a moon for madness and the greed of the flesh.

Ava reached for a cloth that dangled from its tarnished hook. As she washed, paint filled the tub in rivers of purple and green. October was the month of Halfa. The avenues outside blazed with checkered lanterns, hung in honor of the bull and his silver hoard. They worshipped him with sex and wine and reams of paper money. If he was gracious, the year would unveil healthy children and bulging wallets.

Below, the light of street lamps and the brawl of traffic pierced the fog. "A fighting ring," she said. Her voice echoed against a ceiling warped by decades of rain. Whose bright idea had that been? It was no wonder Sariel had run. In the pits he would decompose, joint by joint, under the hands of bigger, stronger wraiths.

Water dripped from the rusty faucet. Ava studied her rose-polished toes. When she was a girl, her father had told them stories of the Craftsman, his wheel and clay, and all the life that sprang from the flame on his sapphire tongue.

"Our ancestors thought their god would live forever," he said, hair and beard like carded fleece in the glare of the hearth. It was Deliverance Eve, and they were together and happy in the big house along the Orchid Coast. "The witches of old were his heralds, and we his beloved children. But even the Craftsman had an end. His soul was leaking through the wells of this world, into a universe more ancient than the sun-star." He spread his hands, jade bangles bright against his midnight skin. "Without him, the witches could not go on. What is a messenger without a message? They turned to ash along the earth-lines. From their bones came saints and goblins and scheming wraiths." He reached over the heads of her sisters, took his glass from the long table and drained it. "The worlds are falling ever backwards. Deliverance Eve is when our maker vanished, and Deliverance Eve is when the Great Dusk will swallow us whole. We will never taste death again."

Ava draped the washcloth over her face. She willed herself to think fondly of her father, and found that she could not. All that remained of him was an ember of warmth, and the sound of her voice rising over the shouts of her brother and sisters: *Dad—Dad! What about the wraiths?*

"What about them?" His shirtfront was heavy with the smell of tobacco and beer. "Wraiths have no place in the Dusk. When the earth-lines cooled, they spread from their wells and followed the trails of our lust and wrath. They tempt us to sin so they may feast upon our terrible deeds. To be free, we must master the sea in ourselves." His eyes disappeared into the folds of a smile. "That is what the Quiet Rites are for. Two years in fasting and prayer is proof that a knight is the bane of wraiths."

"And after that?" Her hands found his wrist. "It's just two years. Mum says that people live till one hundred now."

The house and its eaves seemed to spin on the point of his answer. He gathered her gently into his lap and said, "Sweetheart, the Knighthood is forever."

Ava splashed the surface of the cooling water. She stood up, felt for the towel by the sink, and dried herself off. As the Emperor Tong discovered profit in the research of alchemists and emptiness in the catechisms of cardinals, he found himself at odds with the Knighthood and his adopted church. Countryside fables, he declared last May, when the names of the household spirits were invoked in the palace at Imrakis. With the old dogma gone stale in her mouth, Ava began to wonder if he was right.

She drained the washtub into a narrow runnel, brushed her teeth and struggled into a grey silk gown. George Sandrino was a doting yarn-spinner, but when war and famine struck, he had sold her to the barracks at a nod from his wife. The memory flickered like a picture show, buried beneath the sleepy rattle of New Dera: a door opening in the marble study, her mother's shoes, suede and flour-white upon the wide blue steps.

"We need to speak, George," said Demetra. "The Emperor Tong and his Imraki bride take their tariffs, and their allies take the rest. Marsal and Anglesea laugh behind their hands at Orchid Coast merchants like us." Her sneer was gaunt as the edge of a sword. "You should have gone rum-running while you could. Even starving folks need liquor."

After that, there was a train ticket, then a platform at the edge of town, and a ship with tattered sails. When she arrived at the barracks, an old captain in a pale green helmet caned her for crying. He did not stop until the floor was speckled with blood. "The Western Throne and the Eastern Church are my parents," her mouth had said, dutiful under the steel rod.

Five doors down, the drunk began to scream about tax collectors and black-market children. Ava slammed her window shut. What would her father have done, if he had known? On restless evenings, she reminded herself of his ignorance. Dry coffers and hunger made choices hard. Her brother was the heir to their shipping company, and her sisters were promised to grooms in Karnak. Only Ava had no prospects or place.

She wrote to them every year on Deliverance Eve, when the moon was frosty and full. Her letters were always friendly, tied with lace and bent around crisp yellow bank notes. Sometimes, she sent other things—a silk scarf, black gold coins, glazed turquoise from the wide shores that ringed the southern deserts. *This is what happens when you turn a Sandrino out into the cold,* Ava thought, each time she sealed the envelope. *She prospers as she pleases.*

Demetra, she knew, collected her trinkets without fail, folding the bills away with fingers that gleamed under amethyst rings. Even in the wreckage of famine, the woman had her priorities. Her father always wrote back. Ava never opened his letters.

In the dull radiance of the mirror, her reflection peered out, cheeks burnished by the heat of the bath. She would be twenty-six next month. This leaky apartment had worn out its welcome. Her pockets were fit to burst, but no land owner here would sell good houses to whores. Soon, there would be enough in that safe to buy a ticket to Babel, where the market welcomed all who had cash. Ava could practice her trade without a revolver in her coat. Her wealth would never be in question.

The runnel belched as its pipes swallowed the last drop of water. She crammed her towel into a broken wicker basket. The gossiping neighbors exhausted her. Her long dance with Ezra Shaw exhausted her.

Outside, the loveseat shrieked against the wooden floor. She thought of Sariel, the passages that spanned shipyards and brimstone fields, and the bleached emptiness of a slipstream draft whose ocean tunnels joined one coast to the next in the blink of an eye. The wraith kingdoms were far away; the Northern Dark was farther still. What must it feel like to wear the weight of an empire around one's neck in iron?

There was a bump and a pause. Ava buttoned up her gown, stepping into the corridor that ran between the kitchen and drawing room. Against shivering ropes of light and mist, Sariel stood, both hands on the velvet chair. He had pushed it against the panes of the balcony doors.

"I wanted to sleep under my birth stars," he said. His eyes were hollow in the dark. "I saw them only twice in the mines. Forgive me if I woke you." The cashmere blanket trailed at his heels, draped loosely over one shoulder.

Ava seated herself before the enameled harpsichord. "Nothing to be sorry for," she said. "Everyone wants a glimpse of the sky." An image of her long-ago self bloomed: a little girl, alone on a train heading east. She wept with no one to quiet her while the snowbound constellations melted above.

Sariel let go of the loveseat. He wandered past the unlit hearth, inspecting the golden candlesticks and seven-star lamps. "Alkaseem crafts," he said, like a student reading verse. "They use alloys of mountain copper. The traders from Karnak say these are hard to come by."

"They were gifts from the Paper House Queen." Ava motioned for him to give her his hands. He crept close and knelt on the rug at her feet. She studied his ruined knuckles. "What happened here?"

"Before the slipstream, there were guards," he said. "I had to fight my way in. I am not strong, you see. They sold me because I have red in my stars. My luck is in blood and war. When I start something, I do not stop."

"That's good. That is the way to be." Ava was surprised to find that they were grinning at each other. "We should patch you up," she said. "I've got gauze in the kitchen."

"No need," he replied. "The wounds will be gone before sunrise."

"Fast healers." Her skin felt like cotton against the hard ridges of his fingers and palms. "Our nearest port is up north, by the bone-fires. How did you find your way this far south?"

*Stray women and bad air.* Perhaps he had followed the scent of sewage, drawn south by the lure of sweat and smoke, and the thousand little cravings crushed into her flesh. The idea festered like rot. Ava did not want Ezra to be right.

"I got lost." Sariel flushed. "This city is a maze. They almost caught me at the graving dock. I am sorry about your door."

Ava sat back, relieved. "Locks can be replaced. You are fortunate. This is the only building on the island that still has an open atrium." She hesitated. "Captain Shaw said you came from Selang. There are no brimstone mines there."

"I grew up in the caves at al-Sarif. That was our home, before the alchemist took us." His words were quick and flat. They did not invite revisiting. Ava let Selang and al-Sarif sink into the gulf behind him.

"There is a story that our proctors tell," she said. "It is of wraiths climbing out of earth-wells."

The fire, banked in Sariel's eyes, flickered and grew, and something wild and thoughtless in Ava answered. "Yes," he said. "We are born in the days of flood, from the taproots of our meridian. It is the noise of your souls that stirs us. It keeps us fed, even when we are thoughts in the mind of the soil."

"And are you hungry now?" She tilted her

head towards him. "This city is full of noisy souls. Bodies in the canals. Ivorywomen and opium jockeys. Prostitutes, like me. You could drain the whole street dry."

"Vampires are tales for children." His mouth twitched around a stifled laugh. "The earth-wells are lightning rods. They catch the echo of your numbered days. We do not feast on humans— only the things created by your minds."

His words fell against each other like abacus beads. She loved their arcane logic more than all the nursery rhymes that twisted wraiths into monsters lurking under bridges and docks.

Slowly, her fingers found his again. Ava peered into the cusps of his face, tracing the blisters and knots in his hands. They were close enough that her breath lifted his curls when she spoke. "Our clerics say one thing. Our alchemists say another. Forgive me if we are confused."

"You are forgiven, Ava Sandrino," he said.

The foghorn of a passing ship reverberated against the mossy walls. A lighthouse flashed upon the rocks. It caught Sariel in its beam, and Ava saw him again, sinew and muscle flowing beneath the flesh of his arms, lips parted over silk-white teeth. She knew the bite of desire when it struck, fierce and unbound by the

Paper House walls.

"The black moon sets before Deliverance Eve," she said. "There is a fever that takes hold of you this month, while you wait for wraith cubs to sprout. You must find lovers to warm your sheets."

He laughed. The sound was splintered and rough. "So, humans are storytellers." When he put his forehead against hers, it was with such care that Ava thought of Paper House gymnasts balancing plates on their invisible tightropes. She kept still, waiting for any sign that he might recoil. "At the end of each night, I lay in the dirt with the wraith who carried my firedamp light. We kept each other warm until she passed to the next mine, and another lamp-bearer took her place. The black moon witnessed my birth. It does not tell me what to do." His voice grew bleak. "I do not belong to the brimstone masters, to the alchemist and her elixirs, or to the slavers in Babel."

"No," she said. "We belong to ourselves."

The tips of her fingers found new wheals and old scars. Questions pooled in her mouth. The scent of copper and earth gathered, rich and heavy, in her hips. She knew that if she stood, she would find the nightgown soaked. When she pulled her buttons loose, cold air broke across her skin, only to vanish under his palms as they filled themselves eagerly with her breasts. His breath came shallow and fast.

"You were a knight," he said. "I heard you speaking with Captain Shaw."

She climbed astride his lap and gripped his jaw between her hands. "Why, Sariel!" She laughed. "Do you take me for a Tong loyalist? I just deceived an officer for you."

His dark eyelashes feathered the bridge of her nose. "The Knighthood runs deeper than an earth-well," he said.

"I'm not Ezra Shaw." She took his lip in her teeth, sliding her tongue against the burning roof of his mouth. The taste of smoke from a midwinter fire unfurled. "A knight despises her own desires," she murmured. "Why play dead when you are alive?"

"Wait." Sariel trembled when her hand slid between his legs. "If someone finds out—wraiths and humans—you will be punished."

"No one's watching." She lounged with her elbows against the floor so that he knelt, enfolded in her thighs. "The brimstone mines are gone. You can do as you please—but only if you please."

The lean arc of his back bowed over her. In the quiet that curled around them, he kissed her until her lips throbbed. She searched for the spring of his want, a cartographer tracing the breadth of his circuits and roads. When the next foghorn bellowed, she gave up. There was no instrument that could chart the tides that moved in his eyes. He was no patron, searching for comfort in bedroom oracles.

With a hitching sigh, Sariel pushed himself inside of her. Ava hissed with delight at the familiar stretch and tug. The rough pad of his thumb grazed her nipple, sending electric streams through the hollows of her ribs. "Ava," he said, tightly.

"It's all right." The words caught in her throat. She ran her fingers along the ridges of his spine, through the blue-black waves of his hair. Her nail caught on the root of an obsidian horn. A red and orange leaf dislodged itself and drifted onto the tiles. Dimly, she thought that she had never seen a wraith with such horns.

Coal-warm hands left sunspots where they went. His hips shuddered against hers. He panted her name like a talisman, until the three short letters stuck and ran together. The wet slap and grind of their bodies sent ripples along her darkest seams. They made her think of tidal pools, unlocked doors, coming home to the banyan trees that lined the wide slash of the Orchid Coast.

In the cloudy murk, her mouth found his. Their teeth clicked together. Sariel cried out, and was silenced by what Ava knew was the nameless unraveling at his center. His hand convulsed around her throat. He quivered and groaned, collapsing with his cheek upon her chest.

She covered the hard edge of his horn with her palm. The swell of her pulse chased his: hammer and anvil in a room made strange by nightfall. *Thank you*, he said, again and again, until it was a sound that might be mistaken for the lungs of the surf.

Above the pier, the steam clocks chimed. Ava rolled onto her side. They faced each other, listening to the din of the city below. His eyes were half-lidded and heavy with sleep.

"The Northern Dark," she said. "I know someone who might be able to get you close. He's a silkworm merchant. Comes and goes as he likes."

From where he drowsed, Sariel frowned. "I was headed for Tesalonica. There are hidden routes in their waters and unmarked boats in their ports. Your slipstreams are guarded by knights. Their roads end at the farthest tropic. There is no sailor willing to go farther than that."

"This sailor is different. He has red in his stars, like you. He is not afraid of the edge of the world." Clumsily, she folded herself against him. "Tesalonica is dangerous, and four days by sea. Why not leave from here, if you can?"

Sariel made a noise that might have been agreement, or doubt. Their limbs met in a jumble that Ava knew was meant for lovers, not wraiths and whores. Somehow, the thought failed to trouble her. She fell into a stupor that was broken by car horns and clocks, and dreamed fitfully of jet-black freighters heading west.

* * *

After sunrise, Ava took the mandolin from its stand and watched while Sariel bathed. The water muddied around him, spangled with foliage, while he used up her good soap and chatted about watchtowers and urchin barrens that he had spied through holes in the slipstream. The bronze strings shivered when she plucked them—three bars in C minor, solemn and quick beneath his tales of strange things at sea. Then, at the foot of her narrow bed, she pulled the gown over her waist and showed him just how she liked it with his fingers and tongue.

She finished quickly, face squeezed into the crook of her arm. His hair made puddles on the floor as he clambered onto the samite counterpane. They kissed, long and slow this time, moving against each other with a tenderness that ached, until both of them lay loose-limbed and spent amidst a riot of cushions.

In the kitchen, she swept up the shards of glass, warmed a plate of peppered rice cakes and drowned them in coconut milk. It felt odd to eat while he watched, so she handed him an empty saucer. Wrapped in a silver towel, Sariel squinted down at the floral conceits. Ava straightened the sleeves of her dress, pretending to read the calendar that hung from her wall. She was leaving on holiday next week. A two-way ticket to Sun Tooth Isle had been tacked onto the edge of a blank white square.

"Hardly anyone talks about entering the Northern Dark," she said, reaching for the kettle that whined upon the stove. She took a slice of lemon from the icebox and poured herself a mug of Darjeeling. "Fugitives who go that way are never seen or heard from again. There are colonies, you know." Her gaze met his over the chipped glass rim. "Wraiths like you, living on the islands south of the Americas."

"They would be caught and killed if I joined them," said Sariel. "The ten of us taken from al-Sarif were test subjects. In Selang, they used us until there was nothing left to use." Some undercurrent, wrathful and dark, took root in him. "Your Empire does not like waste. The survivors were sent to a fighting ring, all of us tagged. The iron in my veins will kindle one week from now, and the alchemist will feel my presence, wherever I am in this world."

The words, *test subjects*, turned like anchors against her heart. Wraiths, she knew, were auctioned in batches to laboratories in every country. They were disassembled and rearranged, reduced to pieces and parts so the Empire could see what transformations might be wrought on a living body.

Gingerly, Ava settled her mug on the writing desk. "What about the Landless Kingdoms? Tracking metals don't work beyond your borders."

"I am a fever ship child." He studied his feet. "I have never seen the Landless Kingdoms. Those who leave are not permitted to return. It is the law. My brothers and sisters were sold after the rains came. We know the names of our cities and the signs of the river ghosts, but to come home is out of the question."

Ava was silent. She had seen the floating spires in picture books, soaring out of the amaranth petals that flowered along the meridian. She wondered what Sariel would have been if the fever ships had never come. A monsoon king, perhaps, feeling for storms that would burst the fabled banks, or a numerologist with infinity on the brain. The measureless equations that defined the worlds were the domain of geomancers and wraiths alone.

"So," she said, "the Northern Dark it is."

"There is nowhere else for me." His hands tightened around the saucer, and for a moment, she feared for the safety of her brindled porcelain. "The Northern Dark is what I choose. I will not die before their firing squad, and I will not dig for brimstone at the word of an overseer. I was not good at it, anyway. They told me I did not have the nose."

"Never mind skill." She snorted and blew into her tea. "My mother sold me to the barracks, and my father let her. I might have made a passable knight. I didn't care to be one."

Sariel lifted his head. One of his cowlicks had dried. It stuck out like a third horn. "Captain Shaw," he said. "Were you given to him?"

"No. I chose him." Ava was startled by the sound of her answer. "We were friends at first. He was brave and loud and rude. I wasn't some Orchid Coast castoff when I was with him." The words felt distant and strange. She had never spoken them before. "His parents, of course, are from Sturling-on-Rhone. Old money. They were furious when the proctors told them. Didn't want their son falling in love with some greedy slag from under the Capricorn line." The drink broiled her tongue when she took a sip.

"Love." Sariel repeated it exquisitely, like a scholar resurrecting a long-dead language. "This is why you left your Knighthood."

"When you are young, everything looks like love." She laughed. "Besides, I think it was the Knighthood that left me." January at the train station stole into her mind: Demetra, wrapping her up in a cashmere scarf and pressing fifty lira into the hands of a faceless conductor. Her years at the barracks had been lonely and bleak. Her expulsion almost a decade later was nothing short of a great rebirth.

*Ava Sandrino is full of lust*, the report had read. *What she lacks in discipline, she makes up for in avarice.*

A knight who fell into the Paper House realm was unheard of. Those who recognized her stared openly, and she bore the barbs of their scorn with an upturned nose. Disgraced squires found jobs guarding shipyards, or staffed the checkpoints at which wraiths were vetted for illness and injury. They did not, as Ezra had put it, earn money on their backs.

Quickly, she finished her rice cakes and tea. "I'm off to find my silkworm man," she said. "Can you read?"

"A little." He blinked. "There are handbills and books around the mines. Hundreds, if you know where to ask."

"Then help yourself." Ava waved at the shelves in her drawing room. "It's poetry, mostly, and fiction of the adventurous sort." She tugged her jacket off the coat rack. Its top button wobbled on a pair of fraying threads.

Sariel plunked his saucer down and stood. "You want me to stay here," he said.

"I'll be less than hour. You will need clothes, as well." Ava lifted one of the potted plants from its stucco shelf and unscrewed its false bottom. A few crumpled notes fluttered out. She folded the cash into her sleeve, closed all the curtains, and put on her shoes. When she slid her arms around his neck, the smell of earth surged beneath the tang of honey and soap.

"This will be trouble," he said. His words were cracked and bright. He lifted his hand, fingers creasing the lines of her cheek and mouth.

Ava pressed her lips into his palm. She wanted to kiss him until the Selang alchemist and the brimstone mines were scoured from his flesh. "Here," she said taking the key from her pocket. "It's the only one I have. I'm going to need it when the lock is fixed." She pushed it into his fist. The archer's knot spun on its nickel loop. "Put the chain on the door for now. Do not go anywhere." She waved a finger at him. "And don't open up for anyone but me."

Outside, the hallway stood under a blanket of winter light. Ava shut the door, waited for the rattle of the chain, and cast about for her broken deadbolt. When it was nowhere to be found, she swore under her breath. The ancient thing was dear to her, like the kettle and clock that had come with the flat. The cleaner must have thrown it out during his morning rounds.

Beside the landing, plastic wheels clattered. The neighbor's son sat by the stairs, a toy tractor with a missing roof clenched in his dimpled hand. He looked at her with solemn eyes. From their corner home, his mother watched, bare feet planted upon a reedmace mat.

"Good morning, Inday." Ava cleared her throat, smoothing out the wrinkles in her collar.

"Come here, Caleb," said Inday, holding out a jeweled hand. Cloth bracelets wreathed her arms, and clouds of frankincense stuck to her long red skirt. Her waistband held a deck of tattered cards. She was a reader of fortunes that lay hidden in strange rills of stars. The maintenance staff called her a necromancer, trading tales of her flight across the passage of the Northern Dark. Most of the time, they were only half-joking.

The child dropped his broken toy and stumbled to his mother. She snatched him up under the arms and swept him close against her hip. In the slate-grey sun, they looked like two people connected at the waist.

"The knights were here," said Inday. "Asking after a wraith."

"Yes, I know. They were at my door, too." Ava gave the staircase a pointed glance. Their last conversation had been a spat about the hours that she kept, and the late-night volume of her untuned harpsichord.

Rosary beads quaked around Inday's neck. She straightened the mat with her toe. "Funny," she sniffed. "I did not think you of all people would be home before sunrise. Best get your lock fixed as soon as you can." She deposited her son onto their tiled hall and closed the door behind her. The tractor lay on its side, glinting under the dingy skylight.

Sweat pricked the yellow weave of her dress. There were rumors that the Knighthood kept a string of civilian informers, with eyes that ran from Cape Serendip up to the highest tropic. Anyone who believed this in earnest was mad, and yet, there was no shortage of believers. She might have returned to her flat had it not been for the thought of Inday, watching through the peephole. Ava hurried onto the landing and hoped that Sariel had the good sense to stay silent and still.

The north tower was held together with pockmarked plaster and wallpaper that exhaled tobacco and mold. On the ledge of a second-floor window, the Tong moon hung over a crude sketch of a three-legged donkey. The writing beneath was a wild scrawl: *Usurpers and pretenders return to your tents. Long live House Imrakis!*

The words disgorged from there. *Three hundred years of foreign rule*, they said. *House*

*Tong devours House Imrakis; Awaken, Lady Imrakis, and expel the nomads.* Obscenities done in knifepoint mottled the ruined surface, following the banister down into a blue court-yard that parted around a snow-heavy sky. Empty window boxes and bags of garbage lined the shallow gutters. She walked past bands of men and women smoking on their stoops and ducked under a wood-paneled arch. Cheap fly-ers streamed from the slats of a garden shed. They warned people to travel in pairs and carry lamps after dusk: this year, the hide-behinds roamed the city, restless at their bone-fires.

Her heels echoed down the tilting steps. All the streets lay wrapped in fog that rose from cisterns and sewers. The brume crawled between domed roofs and houses, plummeting into a cradle that held rows of ships docked at the lip of the Climbing Sea.

Fifty years ago, New Dera had not known fog. It was windy and dry, sand from the Has-sani Desert blowing in with the lightening that crackled in spring.

"The newspapers say it's all this mining for brimstone," Ezra had told her, staring out of a barracks window. A pitcher of chilled brandy sat between them. "Anti-Tong sentiment, if you ask me. Our weather was changing long before they broke the soil at al-Sarif."

"What if it's true?" Ava filled his glass, the pitcher slick and sweating in her fist. "I read a journal piece last night. It said that the flood in Sukarta had unnatural origins."

"Geomancer babble." Ezra scoffed. "The earth-wells are expanding as we speak. Brimstone seals the cracks. If all it takes is a bit of rock to keep our cities standing, then let them drill."

"They made jewelry from brimstone once. My mother had boxfuls of bracelets." She lined their tumblers up side by side. "Our cities can stand on earth-wells, you know. The geologists say so. I heard that the holes being sealed are otherworld gateways."

Ezra brayed with laughter. Heads turned. "Ava," he wheezed. "Do you believe every nonsense story told to you?"

"It was on the radio," she muttered, face hot. "There are caches of ivory and opium along the coast of every continent. It can't all be coming through the Northern Dark."

Little by little, he composed himself. "You're not in the dunes anymore, girl," he said, tearful with mirth. "You can sing your songs about camels and sand where the proctors can't hear, but don't mistake this city for your backwater. There is one off-world passage, and unless you're a geomancer, it only runs south."

Behind her, the ululating honk of a four-door automobile sounded. She stood aside as it clattered along the narrow road, its single working headlight flat against the fog. As it passed, a young man in a wide-brimmed hat leaned out of the back seat. "Hey, mademoiselle," he shouted. "Suck my dick for a tenner?"

Before Ava could reply, he flung an empty beer can at her, and the automobile bumped around the corner. The crumpled aluminum landed at her feet. Sourly, she kicked it aside. His face was familiar: he was a medical student who visited the Paper Houses dressed in the colors of his college. He skulked outside the walls each night, with never enough money to put into the waiting hands of the white-robed brokers.

Briskly, Ava walked east. The domes and colored walls narrowed into clay-fired dwellings and canvased market stalls. Where the road became an alley, a fishing house stood, long stilts visible under its bright pink steps. Illegal goods stood in rows, ready for sale behind a quartet of rusty bars: heroin, star iron, amber jars filled with foaming aether. She climbed to where a pot of indigo marjoram stood on the sill.

"Dzemila," she called, rapping upon the chipped ceramic. "Is the tailor in?"

There was a murmur of cloth. A short, red-haired girl appeared, standing on her toes to see out the window. "Dad's sick," she said. "You need something?"

"A quarter ounce of khat and one of the men's outfits that came on the Babel skid. I don't want that garbage they send from Skeleton Lake." She counted out a handful of notes and slid them through the bars. "Medium, I guess. Nothing too fancy."

The girl showed her teeth like a goat spoiling to bite. "Your customers are frisky," she said. "Has this one gone cold on women?"

"Mind your business." Ava waved the cash at her.

Dzemila gurgled with laughter and counted the notes. "I shall return." She folded herself into a mocking bow.

Across the way, a concert of whistles and howls broke out. The people who loitered by the vault of a faded chapel beckoned and clapped. They saw her each evening, walking in velvet scarves beneath the gun of an enforcer. Then, they did not dare make a sound.

"Hey, Paper House Girl," one of them sing-songed. "Don't you know it's Sunday? Enough work! Come to lunch with us. You can sit on my lap!"

"Lunch is a hundred lira," Ava barked. "I don't think you could buy a meal worth half!"

A boy amongst the group spat and straightened his belt. "Did you want to say that again, Orchid Coast bitch? Or is it Kestel you're from?" He laughed. "All sounds the same to me."

"You're not deaf, are you?" Ava pointed over the roof of the chapel, heart racing. "Madame Rummage looks after her employees. Now, piss off, before she sends someone to break your face."

"Employees," the fellow roared. His comrades dissolved into a chorus of jeers, but they let her be. Even the opium jockeys of New Dera went still at the name of the Paper House Queen.

Dzemila returned with a little bag of khat, a crisp white shirt, and trousers cinched together with a pair of dark blue braces. "Making friends, I see." She wrapped them into a sheet of onionskin and slid the package through the bars. Ava snatched it up and hurried down the broken steps.

As she passed the vaults of Saint Genesius,

beggars stirred at her feet. They called for alms, faces hidden in the hoods of their brilliant prayer rags. Ava emptied her coins into an outstretched bowl, pushing through their ranks until the buildings dwindled beneath a massive wall. Vines ensnared it, tracing the path of carvings that had been made long before the ascendancy of the Church and the House of Tong.

At a portal that bristled with the head of a foaming she-wolf, Ava stopped. She leaned hard upon the yawing muzzle. The granite slab swung open. Beyond its arch, the Paper Houses sprawled, red and black tents that towered over unlit taverns. There was no one about but a street sweeper, making her rounds in the company of a thin red dog. Ava shoved her hands into her worn-out pockets and strolled down the rotting planks of Highwater Place.

The old quarter had been falling into the sea for decades. Its former landlord had petitioned the city to have it moved north, but in the tailwind of a building frenzy, the governor would not hear of it.

"New Dera is changing," he had announced. "Brothels do not belong within five miles of good houses."

Highwater Place ended in a hanging bridge.

Ava picked her way across, the surf below hissing into an inlet that harbored wishing spirits and the nests of giant snakes. Nothing had changed. The collection of flats that she called home was a slum, and the bone-fires still roared, beacons of sickness and want. The governor's good houses crowded, unused, around the same grimy haunts.

Breathless, Ava made the steep climb up a limestone path, into a cul-de-sac sheltered from the wind. The Cloud and Cog slouched in its hollow under the sign of the broken jug. Its drooping eaves and blackened smokestacks were sweet with the scent of pink tea and baking bread. Where the dock and awning opened over the long, black jetties, Oliver Lake sat, a clay pot and cup steaming beside him. Under his crooked nose lay a map encased in glass. Tiny numbers leaped back and forth along its lines of latitude, while the stars in their seasons ambled by.

"Red Hag, Oliver," said Ava, settling into the high-backed chair beside him. "When was the last time you shaved?" She listened to the drum of his nails against the map and waited patiently while he ignored her.

Firebrands shifted in the iron censer at their backs. He glanced at his wristwatch, chestnut eyes crinkling with laughter. "Well, do you like it?"

Ava studied him through a wash of cinders. An angry burn peeked over his satin cuff. She knew better than to ask about it. Oliver was forever vanishing and reappearing with injuries of every sort, and he delighted in accounting for them as inventively as he could.

"Gambling in Sawshoe," he explained last month, the left side of his face swollen and purple. "You should see the loser." The week after, he had turned up at her flat with his arm in a sling. "The locks on those Germanian chastity belts are surprisingly loose," he said, sock-clad feet resting on her coffee table. "Things got rough. The diplomat's wife was crazy for me."

"You dumb shit," she replied, not bothering to point out that chastity belts were Tong propaganda, and that Germania did not send or receive diplomats.

He claimed to be younger than her, although she put little stock in his bag of tales. They had met four years ago under the Queen's Tent, where he had beamed into a scree of blue opium. "Hello, darling," he said. "Ever had a silkworm dealer?"

"Twice." Her lips pursed around a smile. "Silk's not so rare these days."

He snickered and kissed her soundly, as if they were privy to some hidden joke. When it was done, she refused his payment, sipping brandy and watching while he dressed. They had never taken each other to bed again.

Ava liked his company, but he was a distant and unsuitable lover. She had no doubt that he was from across the Northern Dark. His accent was queer, and he spoke of places and gods that belonged to the off-world townships. His papers declared him a merchant sailor, but he knew nothing of silkworm eggs, and there was no vessel registered to his name.

In the kitchen above, glass shattered. "Ava Sandrino," said Oliver, drumming his fingers against the arm of her chair. "Answer me. Do you like it, or not? There's a new film out today. It's a documentary about those botanists chasing living rocks in the desert. I was going to ask if you'd be seen with me."

Beneath his pinkie, an ice storm raged across the southern pole. "It looks like you've got fleas." Ava scrubbed carelessly at the stubble on jaw. "I suppose it'll keep the pickpockets away. The cinema draws more crowds than an opium den."

"You're a misanthrope, Sandrino." Oliver topped up his cup and pushed it at her. "Sometimes, I wonder how you do your job."

Ava sniffed at the battered vessel. Notes of honey and apple winked under the bite of wine. "Everyone is different in the dark," she said. "I'm the best that Madam Rummage has."

"And she knows it." He nodded. "All this business she has you wrapped up in—money launderers and ivory smugglers—it's nothing good. Rummage gets fortunes for the sort of information she brokers. She should hire a professional operative."

"Like you?" Ava tilted the cup at him. "I took home more cash in six months than I would have in five years. Think about that when you speak of fortunes."

"Huh. At least she pays for the extra enforcers." He tightened the strap of his watch. "The fake passports seem a bit much, don't you agree?"

"You're not really one to talk, Ollie." She looked at him, pointedly. "It's not all bad. I get some travelling done for free. You should see what she makes the scullery maids do."

"Iberian spies on Monday?"

"Latrine duty on Friday," replied Ava.

"It sounds like more trouble than it's worth— and I don't mean the latrines." His eyes followed the ice storm as it disappeared, going up in a dull white haze. "If that's the career you want, you should do it proper. Rummage is short-changing you. I know a company in Karnak that will pay you triple what she does."

"You keep your company in Karnak." She brushed the beveled glass of the map. New Dera was where Demetra Sandrino had dropped her, and she would exit on her own. *Growing flowers in permafrost*, Dad had called it.

"Oliver." Ava took a draught of wine. "I need a favor."

"Good Lord. You got laid last night." He lifted the clay pot in a toast and drained it without a breath.

She glared. "How did you know?"

"You have that look." He bent his head towards her, close enough that she could see the broken blood vessels in his nose. "Like a pregnant seal." His eye tooth flashed. "So, where did you find him? Is he staying at your flat?"

For a long moment, Ava said nothing. They traded bedroom stories all the time. It was a game: the lewder, the better. Now, the memory of Sariel, wide-eyed in the glow of the lighthouse, made her pause. "The Northern Dark." She lowered her voice. "You go home once in a while, don't you?"

"Home is on Driftwood Way," he said. "You know that."

"If it was, I would have seen it by now." She put a hand on his wrist, glancing quickly over her shoulder. Behind them, a red jay chortled from its roost on the rim of a gourd vase. "You're not like Inday," she said. "The Northern Dark is closed to her. I know you have contacts along the frontier waystations. The slipstreams here are monitored day and night, but people like you—they come and go as they please." She could not bring herself to meet his gaze. "Four years, Ollie. I haven't asked you for a thing."

The jay continued to sing. In the kitchen, a symphony of pots and pans resounded. Oliver dragged his chair close. "I'm listening," he said.

"You are a saint above saints." Ava kissed the burn at his cuff. "I have a friend who needs to disappear into the Northern Dark. I'll pay you whatever you want."

Oliver went still. Beneath the string of birdsong, he asked, "Is this the friend you've taken to bed?"

"Yes. He is a wraith."

"Jesus, Ava." Above them, the half-ring of a daytime moon sliced its way through the fog. He inspected the dregs of the pot, lit a cigarette and smoked it down to the butt before speaking again. "This is the wraith the House of Tong is looking for, isn't it? The one that escaped into a slipstream. Don't look surprised." His hand slid the map aside. The edge of a newspaper crinkled and curled. Ezra Shaw's armored shoulder and slicked-back hair appeared, caught in the light of a flashbulb. "Twenty four-hour presses. That's what I love about this world."

Under the border of the photograph, a headline stood in heavy block letters:

## FLESHBLOOD WRAITH ON THE LOOSE
### NEW DERA KNIGHTS ISSUE WARNING

In the distance, the beam of a lighthouse flickered, and the daytime moon vanished from sight. "Fleshblood wraith," she said. "What is that?"

The cigarette smoldered between his lips. He stubbed it out against the scarred countertop. "He didn't hurt you, did he?"

"Do I look hurt?"

"You recluse." Oliver leaned back, tipping his chair at a dangerous angle. "Your disinterest in current events is alarming."

Ava searched for a retort, only to realize that she had none. Her month was stitched together with rain and the steady din of the Paper Houses. At home, she drowned herself in brandy and books. The radio had sat mute for almost a year.

Below them, the surf broke. "I've been busy." She rubbed at the ache in her temples. "October is the only month we're allowed to perform in public squares."

"Free songs?" Oliver clicked his tongue. "You said only novices have to give those away."

"Madame Rummage is superstitious. We must look pious." Ava put her chin in her hands. "She'll never admit it, but I see the paper goblins she keeps in her robes. She thinks the tent is haunted."

Oliver lit another cigarette and squinted into the soot. "Wraiths are an evolutionary marvel," he said. "They feed on all the things we leave behind—molecules of fear and want and rage and hope, racing down the earth lines and into wells. They speak without words. They can compel each other to act, if they're strong enough. It works on humans, too, but only under extraordinary circumstances. Now, your wraith is special." He blew smoke rings into the cold and held two fingers over his head. "Bet you've never seen one with horns like that."

"You insult me," she snapped. "I've never had

anyone between my legs who I didn't want there."

"Peace, Ava. I am sorry." A muscle twitched in his neck. "The colleges are right about brimstone. This sort of mining is not without consequences."

"The alchemists have barometers. Their readings turn up nothing." Ezra Shaw and his mocking laughter boiled up in her thoughts.

"And yet, Sukarta continues to flood—a highland between dry cliffs." Oliver propped his cigarette up against the map. "The weather is changing. So are the plants and the rocks. Wraiths don't bear children. They grow out of cracks along the meridian, and when they do mate, it is entirely for pleasure. Fleshbloods were a fairy tale until now." His hand made circles in the air. "They put babies inside of each other. They put babies inside of human women. Hope you used a rubber."

The noise inside the teahouse dimmed. A memory of heat and the taste of smoke returned. From a distance, she felt the slide of Sariel's thighs against hers. "Where did you hear this?"

"Medical journal from Jaipur." He picked up his cigarette and took two long drags. "A human woman from Blackwater gave birth to a red-eyed child. The scientists there are beside themselves, and the alchemist here wants to see if she can replicate such a birth. Your wraith was given to a laboratory in Selang. After a year of breeding experiments, the good doctors gave up. The survivors were shipped to the Americas. When they autopsied one of the females, they discovered she had been pregnant. The father was recalled halfway to Anglesea. Your lover was a dad." He slid the empty pot towards the edge of the counter. "He probably doesn't know what he is to the alchemist, or to the House of Tong. This is big. These fleshbloods are a problem."

In the path of the flaming censer, Ava felt the teeth of the October chill. Blackwater was an off-world town. The presence of wraiths was astounding. "A problem? Why?"

"Think about it." Strands of his dirty hair tickled her face. "Each winter, Tong slavers take their harvest from the shores of the Landless Kingdoms. They have done so for almost a century. There are only so many earth-wells. It's the same number every year, and if it isn't, they cull what they don't need. Uncontrolled breeding is frightening and new."

Ava knew that this city was hers, whether she liked it or not. Her throat was filled with its mist and smoke, the sigh of its waves and the rattle of its slow-moving traffic. But when she sat alone at night, she imagined her father, stepping off the train with the Orchid Coast in his suitcase. In her mind, he would wander through the foyer and into the drawing room, running his fingers over the silver candelabra and heartwood tables. "You've done well for yourself," he would say, before all of the fine things that she had won through the force of her body and work.

Now, her mother's voice eclipsed his. "Our girl is a whore," it murmured. "She's gone and let a wraith put its whelp inside her."

Oliver seemed to glean something from her expression. "I'm all in, darling," he said. "We'll sort it out."

"His name is Sariel." Ava stared into the clay cup, inspecting the coarse rinds that lay stuck to each other against the crosshatched bottom. "It never sat right with me, you know. Wraiths in the brimstone mines, the fighting rings, the fever ship children. We were afraid of them, so we put them in traces and put them to work."

"Afraid?" Oliver grinned. "The Landless Kingdoms were swimming in blood. We got our foot in the door while they were divided and weak, offered help, and took the lot. The slave trade is thriving, and Houses Tong and Imrakis—united under one sacred banner, long may it fly—have been stroking their cocks over a hoard of brim-stone ever since."

"A labor of debt," she mused, "for saving wraiths from themselves. That's what the bish-ops say."

"Whatever fiction suits them." His fingers waltzed across the map. "Revisionism at its fin-est. The Tong worshipped other gods and lived by other names—conquerors with business minds, you see." He tapped his forehead. "There were no holy revelations at the gates of Imrakis. The Imraki king had powerful enemies, and the Tong were tired. It's a long way from the Bahrei Steppes. Alliance looked better than siege, and I must say, the old union has aged quite well after three hundred years."

"Enough," said Ava. "You like to hear yourself talk, Ollie. That's why the women never stay. I'm not religious, and I'm certainly no loyalist."

"Ah, but you are superstitious, just like Madame Rummage." Behind them, the red jay squawked. "The Northern Dark is still within reach of the knights. They'll appeal to the geomancers. There is a treaty. Your wraith will have to find the near-est township and lie low. A month, maybe two. After that, he can petition the One O'clock King for entry into the black-market cities."

"He has no trade they would want." She frowned. "What would he do there?"

"They will find something to want, and he will find something to give." Oliver chuckled. "The throne has a long memory, sweetheart. It's the only way to properly disappear."

"The Pit Lords rule the black-market cities." Ava leaned towards him, fingers splayed over the pot of honeyed wine. "The One O'clock King is a myth. No one has ever seen him."

"The man is real, I assure you." His mouth twisted into something that was not quite a smile. "He is an idealist, at least in name. No slaves, no second-class citizens. He's a rogue geomancer. His palace is built on the backs of fugitives." He stretched and yawned. "I know every deer trail that runs between here and the Northern Dark, but I'd like to meet this wraith first. I have to figure out who it is I'm taking onboard."

"He's at the flat," she said.

Both of them stood. Oliver pulled a thin wallet from his pocket and pressed a few notes onto the riven wood. The waitress counted them out, licking her thumb as she went. "Hey, Lunatic," she said. "This is less than half of what you owe for the week."

"I'm good for it." Oliver waved the wallet imperiously. "There's more where that came from."

"Oh?" The woman's eyebrows made an angry point. "Where is it, and where has it been for all of White Bull month? You should own this place by now!"

Ava listened while they argued. A blighted, thoughtless piece of her worried that he might change his mind. Meddling in the sale and transport of wraiths was a capital crime, but he had always been a devotee of the unorthodox.

Oliver emptied his wallet of a few foreign coins and took his jacket from the clawed ear of the chair. "I'll be paid up by Thursday," he said, tapping the glass-covered map against the counter. It shattered, turning into bands of dust. He got one arm into his coat and rounded the corner into the fog.

Ava gathered up her onionskin package. The waitress put a hand on her wrist. "Eight-hundred lira," she said. The gold ring in her septum wobbled over her upper lip. She shoved a handful of damp hair out of her eyes, adding the clay pot to the stack of plates that seesawed in her left hand. "Tell your friend that's how much he owes. The owner lets him rob us blind, but this is simply too much. We run a café, not a charity."

"He keeps the hide-behinds away, doesn't

he?" Ava pulled her collar around her ears.

"You have never seen a hide-behind, sweet girl. Except for the bone-fires, they are terrified of light." The waitress spat onto the grass-edged pavement. "This is not his private study. He's been going over that map for weeks. I want him gone. Northern Dark folk are bad news; whatever they're running from runs them down in the end." The stack of clay teetered. She righted it and gestured brusquely at the door.

Ava joined Oliver in the cold. He was perched upon the top step, rearranging the trinkets hidden in the pockets of his coat. "She likes me," he said, motioning for her to follow him.

"Pay your tab, Oliver," said Ava. "This is Wren Avery's joint. She's a good woman, but she'll want her money soon."

"She'll get her money." Loose shale slid under their feet. "Besides, I keep the hide-behinds away."

Halfway to the bottom, a child squatted by the cliff face. Her gloved hands pulled up snarls of winter weeds. She stopped to stare at Oliver, eyes wide at the sight of his houndstooth clothing, buttons and zippers sewn into all the wrong places. He gestured while he spoke, drawing shapes that underscored the names of ships, slipstreams and planets. His undone sleeves lifted, revealing flocks of birds resting in ink under his skin. Their pinfeathers were joined with rows of characters that Ava knew nobody in this world could read.

They took the road that slid along the jetties, turning north onto a bridge whose lion-faced rails sagged beneath garlands of shriveled flowers. Between the gutters of Aurumine Street, a crowd had gathered. They whispered behind their hands, watching as a line of green-clad knights raced up the byway that wound past a moldering gate.

A woman with a long pipe tugged at the scarf of a hunchbacked beggar. "It's those flats by Agia Idin," she said. "Bet you twenty lira it's an ivorywoman. They've been coming out of the Northern Dark in droves this year."

Ava yanked open the gate. Her hair streamed with saltwater. "That's my place," she said. The arms of the crowd closed over them as they broke into a halting run.

The khat and clothes were crushed against her chest. Her feet flew, soles snapping against the iron walkway that arched over a string of sewage pipes. She passed Dzemila's shop and its run-down chapel, bursting through choke-points clogged with bicycles and automobiles.

Oliver shouted. A driver honked and swore. Ava did not stop until she saw the plaster peak of her building and the belly of its atrium, held open with cinderblocks. A complement of knights waited beside a black lorry. Ezra Shaw stood between the wooden gates. She limped up the causeway, fingers buried in the onionskin, and willed her breathing to slow.

"Captain," she said, thinly. "You're back."

"Ms. Sandrino." He held out a thin, leather-bound book, glancing quickly at Oliver Lake. "I believe these are yours."

Ava pretended to inspect the raised print that ran along the volume's spine: *A Collection of Western Poetry*. Her tarnished key lay atop its cover. "You must be mistaken, Ezra." She raised her hand like a shopper warding off cheap market goods.

"That's 'Captain Shaw,' and I don't think I am." His words grew sharp and dry. He turned his back to the lorry and its knights and thumped the book against her shoulder. " 'There are no witches where we have gone,'" he recited. " 'No silver-plated men; no silk women.' It has your name on the second page."

Her face flooded with warmth. She had read that verse to him in an empty guardroom, glutted with worship at each breath he took in the hollow of her arms.

"I never did you wrong, Captain Shaw." Ava lifted her head, cheeks incandescent. "Sorry that my expulsion was a disappointment."

Ezra dropped the book and key between them. A crack appeared in the blank wall of his face. "The Paper House Queen is no champion of yours," he said. "My father knows people. There are job openings in every shipyard along the coast."

"Security detail?" Anger broke her voice. "I get five times the wage of a barracks dropout. Why would I want to watch pineapples in the rain for less?"

"Money and villas in Babel," said Ezra. "That was all you could ever think about. Your parents should have sent you to an East County brothel."

"Don't talk about my parents." She kicked the book at him. One of its pages tore under her heel. "There was a time all you could think about was Babel, too. Getting caught scared you into being a good little knight. Now, move along. I'm going home."

"You're going to jail in Selang," he said. "You lied to an officer and sheltered a runaway. Forensics collected your deadbolt during our sweep last night. It's a relic. The only key that fits is the one we found hanging from the creature's neck." He bent close. "A wraith, Ava? And a fleshblood, at that! Did you let yourself think he was human?" His fingers lifted the onionskin. "Are these for him? Beasts don't wear braces, you know."

Something scathing and hot leaped in her throat. She caught sight of Oliver, waving at her to be silent. In the gathering wind, her ears were filled with the dull clank of steel.

Flanked by the gates, Sariel stood, stooped under the weight of aether-bright chains. Blood poured from his nose and mouth. His left eye was swollen shut. The trousers at his waist were a size too large, held in place by a thick plastic belt. Behind him prowled a flame-haired wraith. The Tong Family collar sat high on her neck; her gold-flecked eyes followed each flicker of movement.

"Son of a bitch fought us," said the knight who held his tether. "He got away twice. We had to use Red here."

Ezra began to reply. The sound of his voice was a dim and far-off rumble. Ava stared, word-less, at Sariel. He said nothing and looked away.

In the glare of the atrium's light, she glimpsed Inday, long tresses scraped into an unforgiving knot. She looked small amongst the ranks of knights, her son a tangle of knees and elbows in her lap.

"Listen." Oliver was at her ear, beard rough against her skin. "My mother knows a barrister—"

"Not now." She nudged him aside and marched to where Inday sat, stiff beneath the ragged awning. Her white knuckles were laced around her son. "You called them," said Ava. "You miserable wench. You've never been able to stomach the idea of living next to a whore. You sold me—to *them*—who would send you back into the Northern Dark—"

"You are a fool." Inday tightened her hold on Caleb. "Why would anyone from beyond the Northern Dark even look at a knight?" She sneered. "Maybe in Selang, we will be cellmates, you and I."

The rage drained from Ava, leaving her hollow and slouched. "You're under arrest," she said, dull with shock. "Why?"

"Mrs. Espinosa-Sullivan saw us coming." Ava jumped when Ezra spoke. "We caught her letting the wraith out through the rooftop door. No need for restraints—Ms. Sandrino will do as she's told." He crooked a finger at the attending knights. "This way, Mrs. Sullivan. Your son can go with Officer Yang. He will be well cared for in your absence."

Furiously, Ava rounded on him. "She's not letting you take her kid."

There was a ripple of motion. Ezra waved at the others to remain as they were. "To think," he said, under his breath. "I almost lost the Knighthood for you—some breeding bitch from where the dung beetles grow."

From a distance, she heard Oliver say her name. There was a new and frightening terseness in his voice. She ignored him, driving her finger into Ezra's chest. Her breath spooled between them like fishing wire. "Well, you kept the Knighthood, and then some. Are you satisfied? Stealing children from their parents is a piss-poor show of force, even for you."

The clang of iron rang over the grate of engines and wheels. Sariel sat down between the jaws of the lorry. His silence felt like hearth fire in her ribs.

Before she could blink, Ezra tore the onion-skin from her arms and trampled it beneath his boot. He crushed her wrist, dragging her into the circle of his celadon sleeves.

"Hey," barked Oliver. The sound of his protest dimmed under the grind and roar of the city.

"You greedy cunt." She saw the birthmark that scored the Captain's brow. "Silk jackets and bedwarmer wraiths! Nothing is ever enough for you."

"Forgive me, My Lord." The words oozed between her teeth. "I forgot that I am not meant for finer things. Bored, spoilt boy, looking for adventure in the barracks." Her lip curled. "Some of us are born hungry. Others eat money for breakfast."

"Yes," he said. Her bones creaked beneath his fingers. "We all have our place. Wraiths, dogs, and whores." He called out roughly to Oliver. "Does she complain to you, my friend, about having to carry a gun? Does she weep because of the drunks that pester her at the Paper House gate?" His laughter blared above her. "Some crazed admirer broke into her flat last month, you know. Filched her cotton slip and nice black shoes. I have the report in my office. That is what happens when the goods are too sweet."

"I'm not your friend, Captain," said Oliver.

"Your gravestone awaits, Ava." Ezra lowered his voice until it boiled between them. "If the scarring sickness doesn't do it, some merchant sailor will. His knife will find your throat after he spends himself inside you. Can't buy your way out of that."

Ava felt her knuckles crack across Ezra's

mouth before she realized that her hand had moved. Her jade ring tore the flesh of his chin. When his gloved fist collided with her face, she saw blooms of purple. The air pulsed with a welter of shouts and crunching metal.

"Fuck," said Oliver Lake.

Sariel tumbled from the van, limbs bent beneath the golden chains. His shoulder clipped the armored wraith and sent her sprawling. "No," he roared, panic and rage twisting into ribbons of fog.

Red scrambled to her feet, the gasp of her greaves loud against the stone. She was a war wraith from the east, bristling helmet hiding the bony prominence of her head. The earth trembled as she sprinted after Sariel.

Nearly twelve paces away, Ezra pulled a black revolver from the holster at his chest. When he cocked the weapon, the sound of the hammer burst in Ava's ears. "So," he said, without looking at her. "You do know each other." The cylinder blushed with the warm light of aether.

"Ezra, stop!" The shout rattled in her throat. There was a hiss and a flash. The bullet left its gun in a slow stream of white.

"Ava," said Oliver. She whirled to face him. His eyes were polished bronze; the veins under his skin glowed with forks of light. "This is an expensive wraith, darling."

A stillness gathered in the air above. His out-stretched fingers caught on an invisible thread. They snapped shut, and the bullet slowed. It vanished inches from its mark, thawing into clouds of yellow smoke. Streams of letters and runes scattered in its wake.

Red flew at Sariel, thudding bodily against him. They went down in a heap of limbs. A chasm of silence rose in the square.

Oliver bent with his hands on his thighs, face creased. "I hope you have a plan," he rasped. "My boss knows what I just did."

From under the awning, one of the knights cried out. Inday staggered towards Oliver with Caleb between her knees. "Geomancer," she croaked. Her face shone beneath a mask of tears and fog. "Do you know my husband? His name is Joseph Henry Sullivan. He is one of yours. Speaks English, like you—yes, I recognize your accent! He is a headman at the breakwater waystations." She tore at his sleeve. "Take me there, please. It is close, but I do not know the way. My son must go home."

Ava felt the axe-blow of defeat. She looked at Caleb, pulled tight against his mother. "No," she whispered. "I had no plans for this."

Captain Shaw spun towards them. "You'll get the firing squad." His mouth was a rictus of rage. "Your guild does not interfere in Tong Family business!" He emptied the revolver of aether and filled it with lead. Golden bullets clicked against the flagstones.

"I wouldn't do that, Captain." The skin of Oliver's face was waxy and drawn, but his eyes were warm and brown again. "Put it away. I could drop you all dead, just like that." His palms coming together resounded through the rain-flecked air. "Killing you is both illegal and conveniently quick."

Ezra paled, then flushed. His weapon clattered against the broken stones. "The wraith is imperial property," he spat. "There is a treaty between our government and yours. You know what the punishment for theft is."

"Of course." Oliver's voice was flat and cold. "A handler will send my balls to Imrakis in an agarwood box." He shrugged. "So, take the wraith. He's yours."

Ava's mouth went dry. "Oliver," she said. "You can't—"

"I like my balls, Ava." He held up a hand. "We concede, Captain, but my friend and Mrs. Sullivan come with me."

"What does it matter?" Ezra looked murderous. "You're dead, anyway. For threatening a knight, your guild will extradite you. They won't give asylum to a thieving whore and a lying fortune-teller."

Oliver looked down at his undone cuffs. "Oh, Captain Shaw," he said. "Don't you know? I'm like you. My dad is a Lake, and my mum is a Barrowcrown. Real big names east of Blackwater." He did up the first two buttons. "Punishment, yes. Execution, however, is out of the question. I'm their darling boy." He grinned. The third button found its hole. "Well? Do you accept our terms?"

"You're insane." The captain lifted a shaking hand at them. "Nobody walks away from the murder of a knight."

With his hands in his pockets, Oliver bent at the waist. "Be sure, now. This is nothing to take your chances on."

Silence stretched between them, dented only by the scratch of Sariel's breath, rolling out from under the chest of the war wraith. Finally, Ezra snapped his fingers at the knights that ringed the grounds.

"What has happened here is treason," he said. "We will return. If you are caught attempting to leave the city, you will be shot on sight."

"Then I must not be caught." Oliver stood up straight, just as the rain turned to sleet. "Sandrino." He gestured magnanimously towards the atrium. "Mrs. Sullivan."

Once, long ago, Ava had gone swimming with her sisters in the River Ur. They had splashed in the shallows while she dove between the barges and stilt houses, limbs tugged southwards by currents hurtling through. She felt glassy and weightless again, trailing after Inday and Oliver. When she bent to pick up her key, her eyes found Sariel.

"I am sorry," he slurred as Red hauled him to his feet by the steel ring in his collar. Blue veins pulsed beneath her milky skin. "I thought—"

"Sariel." Ava was not sure if she spoke his name out loud. "Why did you do that?"

Blood dripped from a crack in his lip. "They took everything from me in Selang," he said. "All that was good. Anyone who was kind. I did not want them to take you, too."

"Take me where?" She reached for him, then thought better of it.

"Hurry up," one of the knights shouted. Above them, the sky disgorged a torrent of icy rain. They closed ranks around Sariel, bundling him into the lorry as its engine coughed and purred. The war wraith towered above them. She had lost her helmet in the tumult. The downpour turned her hair the color of burnt bricks.

"His eyes are red, like the dust of the star." Inday stood under the arch, suddenly serene. Caleb fidgeted, fingers hooked on her thumb. "This is not the end for him. Come."

The doors thudded shut behind them. With the glare of headlights at her back, Ava slunk into the courtyard, head bowed.

Somebody shouted. People darted along the boardwalk, snatching laundry down from long cloth lines. Dried saffron stood in bushels, the scent of it drifting in plumes through the air. The concrete pores seemed monstrous to her.

"Ava." Oliver stood, foot planted on the step of a metal staircase. He nursed his ribs with one hand. "The north tower, right?"

"Yes," she said. The word fell, legless, from her lips.

Each landing was filled with trays of sorrel ivory, smuggled in by masked women from the north. The dark bones rattled in their ceramic holders as they climbed. When they reached her floor, a blast of diesel and brine gusted towards them. A rooftop door stood open, the storm outside blackening the threadbare carpet.

"Mrs. Sullivan." Oliver stopped in front of Ava's flat, fingers skimming the broken lock. "I'm going to seal the entrance, just in case Captain Shaw decides to get smart. Is there anything you need from your home?"

Inday drew Caleb against the pleats of her skirt. The ring on her thumb was a rain dragon, swallowing the rattle of its own tail. It furrowed his soft cheek. "You have coats, Sandrino," she said. "Warm clothes."

"Yes," Ava replied.

"My husband wires money to accounts in Blackwater and Thrace. I keep the letter of credit in my shoe." She gave them a lopsided smile. "It has been a long exile. I need only to leave."

The foyer was dim and cold. They huddled together, shivering around a glass umbrella stand. Quickly, Oliver slid his thumb across the space where the deadbolt had been. A sprig of light unwound across his palm, and the thin wood of the door began to move. Its planed-down knots stretched and writhed like serpents from a winter nest. Amidst the crack and groan of planks, the lines of timber crawled east. The door vanished. Ava found herself staring at a thick mass of sapwood.

"There," he said, breathless. "Bastard will have a time with that. Don't say bad words," he added, glancing sideways at Caleb. "That's quite the shiner you've got there, Sandrino. Is your icebox still in the kitchen?"

Mutely, she nodded. His shadow disappeared behind the white stucco wall. The catch pan rattled, and she heard him curse.

"There are brined eggs and jackfruits in the kitchen," said Ava to Inday, who regarded her with new-moon eyes. "Sweet rice in palm leaves for the boy. You can sit in the drawing room if you like. Here, follow me."

"Don't touch anything," she heard Inday hiss, dragging Caleb along.

The old lamp hummed. Ava blinked at the couch, off-center in front of the mahogany bookcase. Sariel had been reading. The green blanket was rucked up beneath books filled with poems about the mysteries of love and death, and atlases charting the waterways that split the world. His eyes had stopped on a detail of the highest tropic. Whitecaps and glaciers dotted its sounds. She pictured his fingers tracing an invisible road that ran off the page into a dark that whistled with sleet.

"Inday," she said, before she could stop herself. "Where were you exiled from?"

The woman did not reply at first. She propped her son up on the cushions and stroked his hair until his eyes drifted shut and he slumped against the armrest. "I am from an island full of sun," she said. "It lies six thousand miles beyond the Black-water node. None of your business, of course."

Too tired for anger, Ava nodded. As thunder pealed overhead, she tidied her books, arranging each volume by genre and title. "The wraith," she said, standing on her toes to shelve *The Boatmaker's Song.* "You helped him escape. At least, you tried to. Why?"

"You are nosy today, Ava Sandrino. Why does it matter?"

"You don't like me." Ava forced the book into place. She felt heat swell in the pouch beneath her eye. "I'm a whore, and he's a brimstone beast. Our people tell stories about them. They are like demons, I suppose, from your nine circles of hell."

"Love your enemies."

"I'm not your enemy."

"All of New Dera is my enemy." Inday wedged herself between Caleb and the armrest. By the light of the amber bulb, she looked like a cat with its hackles up. "This rotten city wants my son.

Do you know what the hide-behinds are?" When Ava shook her head, Inday cackled. "They are a curse from the Lord Almighty. The geomancers and the House of Tong play at righteousness, but they are fat because of black market goods. Your Emperor stages raids and arrests. He burns pyres of off-world contraband, then waits at the mouth of the Northern Dark, thirsty for more. No one survives in all the worlds who does not bend their knee to the One O'clock King."

Ava frowned. "The hide-behinds are pests, Inday."

"Enough!" Inday glared. "You should have turned the wraith out. Was it a lover you were looking for?" She tossed her hair. "I see you filling up this empty flat with bodies and books. He will never be true, you know. It is not in their nature. They share one mind. What makes you think that he will know how to share one bed?"

Before Ava could answer, Oliver sauntered into the drawing room, a bottle of beer in one hand and a sack of frozen goat ribs in the other. He crooked a finger at her.

"I didn't say you could help yourself to my drinks, Lake." She gave him a withering look.

"Sorry," he mumbled, draining the bottle. Together, they disappeared into her unlit bedroom. The sound of Inday singing a counting song lagged after them.

Thunder boomed again, and the windows of the water closet shook. Oliver handed her the frozen parcel, set down the empty bottle and stripped off his jacket and shirt. "The sex must have been miraculous," he said, voice muffled. "Your wraith thought Captain Shaw was going to shoot you. In the brimstone mines, raising your hand to a knight means a bullet in the brain."

The expanse of flesh on his back glowed under the cast of a distant lighthouse. Dark bruises bloomed along the knots of his spine, lashing his ribs in black and purple forks.

"Lord Craftsman below," said Ava. "Is this what happens when geomancers do their magic?"

"It's not magic, just a trick of genetics. Not important." He grunted when she pressed the cold pack into his skin. "Each world is attached to the next by clusters of earth wells. Those wells are strung together on lines that make up everything you see. My boss—she can feel it when I alter them without clearance."

"And so, she did this to you?" Ava winced, tending to a violet blotch that spanned the breadth of his shoulders.

"Yes. It's like putting a boot on a tire." She stared blankly at his mirror image. "It marks a geomancer for punishment. It also hobbles me," he said. "Trying any tricks now is going to be exceedingly difficult." He turned around, taking the cold pack from her hand. "Close your eyes."

Ava squinted against the sudden sting of ice. She was gripped with fear. "Oliver," she said. "How does the guild punish geomancers?"

"Without mercy." He laughed. In the tines of lightening that tore the sky, he looked like a goblin on the wall of Saint Genesius. "Don't you worry, darling," he said. "Our surgeons can put a man back together from the dead. Besides, they never give more than you take."

"Ollie." Ava closed her hand over his. "You should have told me. I would never have asked." She knew right away that this was a lie.

"Even the One O'clock King on his black-market throne knows the sale of wraiths is wrong. Besides, there's another thing." He glanced towards the door, where a wedge of yellow light oozed beneath the sill. "Inday Espinosa-Sullivan is one of those Blackwater Brides: a human married to a geomancer. The guild forbids them from conceiving children."

"Why?"

"Strange genes. Some of the half-breeds can do things that we can't—things that are almost magic. The very idea terrifies our governing board."

"Is that why she came to New Dera?" Ava watched as he slid into his shirt, the dark ink on his arms vanishing under satin sleeves.

"The guild disposes of mixed-blood children under the age of one." Oliver made a slicing motion across his throat. "She ran off and gave birth in secret." He opened her medicine cabinet, fumbling for a jar of willow bark. "Jesus, Ava, you really don't move anything around." A single tablet skittered across the bottom. He tilted it into his mouth and washed it down with water from the sink. "Caleb is a geomancer. I can feel it coming off him in waves. His mother is frightened. She wants to get him to his father before he kills someone."

"And Inday?" Ava's voice was a harsh whisper. The ramshackle pipes carried sound into every room. "What will happen to her?"

"The Guild will have her hanged. She is known to them. They have been watching and waiting for years." The words thudded into her chest. His mouth tightened. "Her husband is Joseph Henry Sullivan, a pedophile who stole her from the heart of a slum. She was eleven years old and half-dead from thirst. He kept her around for want of a wife and an heir. Appearances, you know. She's in her thirties now—too old to entertain him. The boy, on the other hand, is just the right age."

"She's giving him to a monster." Her tongue felt parched. "Your guild retains animals, Lake. Won't they punish him, too?"

"Nobody knows the frontier waystations like he does. They'd be hard-pressed to hire a replacement." He folded his collar and straightened his watch. "Inday has no choice. Most regional governments execute or imprison geomancers unclaimed by the Guild, and the Tong love their firing squads. But there is another way—for the kid, at least."

"And what is that?"

"I will see him through the Northern Dark, then on to the Blackwater node that lies beyond. It is watched by many and owned by none. There is an Eighth Pike outpost just two hours south. I can register him there—with Mrs. Sullivan's permission, of course." He stretched his arms and winced. "We'll need a boat out of New Dera. My port pass is no good."

The water closet grew still and stifling. "You'll

take him away from his family," said Ava. "You'll make him a marksman, like you. Oh, hush. I've had you all figured out for a while."

"He has no family, Sandrino. Inday has sisters, but they fear the Guild, just like everyone else. If we don't take him, his father will." Above them, the lightbulbs faltered and buzzed. "It's not so bad, darling. I grew up in the Eighth Pike. Free meals and top-rate doctors."

"Your Eighth Pike is the sword of the Guild." Her heart quickened and leaped. "They beat children until they're loyal. They starve them of food and sleep and throw them away when they get old or sick."

"Ava." Oliver smoothed her curls with his thumb. Shadows moved across the lattice-work of leaves and bones inked upon his neck. "There's not a lot of places for an unattached geomancer to go."

"Except for you," she said. "You told Captain Shaw that you're the same—a marksman by choice. Were you looking for some fun, too, rich boy?"

"No," replied Oliver, unruffled. "I was looking for something, but it wasn't fun."

"Then what?" Heat rushed to her face. She felt like a train skidding to a halt along winter tracks. "Did your mum turn you out because you forgot to dust the good silver?" She lifted her chin. "Who are, anyway? You say you come from money, and you can't even pay your tab at a dockside teahouse."

He rewarded her with a slow blink. "You have been my only friend here, Ava, but some things are for me to know." The flicker of his long eyelashes seemed like a dismissal. "The Eighth Pike is a barbarous world," he said, "but they won't touch him—not like that. There are rules that are enforced on pain of death. In our company, he will see the sun rise on strange worlds. He might even become a commander. What would he get at Joseph Sullivan's? Nightmares, and a future at the helm of some miserable waystation."

"Can't he go with you?" Ava heard the words, staccato with desperation.

"Me?" Oliver peered down his long nose at her. "I have no home. I was sent here to cull the hide-behinds. Saint Genesius has made a passable bed and breakfast, I'll say." He folded his arms. "When my handler's through with me, I'll be in a Florida hostel seeing to the latest war machine. Then, it's the desert for autumn. The guild is buying two tons of al-Sarif brimstone. I won't be around to make the kid flapjacks and eggs before school in the morning."

Ava sagged against the washtub, clasping her hands over her belly. "Why does Inday not send the boy alone? She can save herself, at least. Besides, you said that Blackwater is neutral." Poison, surly and sharp, crept into her words. "Or does your Guild make its own laws about that?"

"Crossing worlds is like visiting Sukarta," said Oliver. "She must declare herself his mother. That happens at the first port, one mile outside of Blackwater." He let out a sharp breath. "It's the most elegant solution. Except for children passing through, they don't ask a lot of questions. Caleb will go to the Eighth Pike. Sariel can find shelter in the township for now. And you? There are stops along the way. Upper Kestel, Karnak, the Americas. The whole world is yours, darling."

"There must be a way for Inday, too. Joseph Sullivan must want to help her. He made half that child."

"Joseph Sullivan is untouchable and unconscionable. The Guild lets him do as he likes. There are marksmen who won't go near the far-flung outposts."

"She loves the boy," said Ava, "more than she loves herself." Demetra and her bloodless face emerged, thin under a fur hat on the platform of a midnight station. The famine had flooded graveyards and hospitals while the Orchid Coast languished beneath a twelve-year winter, but there were families who had held out with less. Her mother had sold Ava before pawning her cheapest ring.

She closed her eyes. Inday and Caleb crossed her mind with joined hands, followed by Sariel, whose thoughts clattered along train tracks running into the Northern Dark. When she looked up, Oliver was staring at her, something relentless and wild on his narrow face.

"I didn't use a rubber," she said. The noise of her confession broke like echoes in a cave. "He's a wraith. They're supposed to be—you know. No scarring sickness. No babies."

"Babies." Oliver touched the low swell of her stomach. "Is that what you want?"

Thunder purled again. Ava pictured her feet in a pair of white shoes, the mistress of an enormous house with a little girl at her skirt. The shoes dissolved, and she stood in the grass with a child at her toes. *I could do a lot better than Demetra Sandrino*, she thought.

"Ollie," she said. "Inday is going back through the Northern Dark. Is it possible for someone like me to go that way, too?"

"Of course." Oliver raised his eyebrows. "Giving birth to a geomancer doesn't make her special. There are paths that only we can tread, and then, there are leaky valves. These are the earth-wells that your priests pretend are gateways to nothing. They are doors into the other-worlds. The Northern Dark is the biggest one of them all. Anyone can access it, but the entrance is almost impossible for all but a geomancer to find." He gave her hips a playful squeeze. "Has New Dera left a bad taste in your mouth?"

"It was just a question." She had many more. Was brimstone really being used to seal the cracks between worlds? What purpose did the guild serve, and where did its edges bleed into the black market, whose presence reached her only through the goods that arrived on late-night ships and morning-bound trains?

Before she could say anything else, Oliver's arms and the whisper of his shirt engulfed her. "Sunrise in twelve hours," he said. He smelled like ash and sweat and beer.

"Sorry about Ezra," she mumbled into his pocket square. "He was a lot different when I knew him. That was before his dad and the Knighthood shoved their holy sword in his ass."

"People like us don't have to explain, darling." His words rumbled through the flesh and bones of her chest. "Not to anyone."

Ava grasped at his words, measuring their weight and worth. In all their time together, she had learned only two things for certain: that he was different, and that he was lonely. Perhaps that was good enough.

"No," she said, at last, and he seemed to exhale. "I suppose that we don't."

\* \* \*

When the night birds sang, Ava traced the streets that ran between steam-powered clocks and ditches, mapping them out against the cracks in her frosted window.

"All prisoners bound for Selang are quarantined first." Her fingers slowed along the western road. "The old governor was a fool, trying to build holding cells so close to the sea. The new governor is too drunk to fix it. They couldn't lay foundations, and those floating cages fill up fast." She bent and rearranged the potted succulents that lined the shelves. One of them was a victim of overwatering, orange blotches spoiling its ocean-green hide.

"Here's hoping we don't contribute," said Oliver. "This plan has more holes in it than a two-bit fishing net. Madame Rummage is a wolf."

"You have never met her."

"I don't have to. Every time she makes a deal, you come out of it by the skin of your teeth. What makes you think she'll do as you ask?"

"Haven't I always done as she asks?" A carmine thorn pricked her thumb. "She is gracious when she wants to be. Besides, every opium jockey from here to Saint Martinsberg lets the old crow take a cut of their wealth—and for what? Only I know why. If that's not debt, it's blackmail."

"Nobody blackmails the Paper House Queen."

"She's not a god, Ollie," snapped Ava. "She needs persuading, is all. We have time. Now that you've meddled, there's collusion involved. It will take Ezra twenty-four hours to draft new arrest warrants, and half a day to have them signed."

"A rousing speech, Sandrino. Madame Rummage is no horseback hero." He laughed without humor. "Inday will need your revolver, at least. If anything happens to us, Tesalonica will be her only available port." He hesitated. "That's something like a death sentence, wouldn't you say?"

"Inday is smart." Ava prodded the swollen flesh around her eye. "She's kept her nose clean and her son fed for years. Tesalonica has unguarded slipstreams. They can disappear while she looks for a slow boat north."

"Every cutthroat and rapist with legs to run ends up there, claiming allegiance to the Ash-and-Bone Queen. There are swindlers posing as geomancers. They sell fake routes into the Northern Dark for ten times the cash you're giving her." He pulled one of her plants into the light and squinted into its puckered spines. "This thing is finished, Ava. Too much water."

"Stop rattling it around." She reached for the red clay pot. His hand swallowed hers.

"If anything happens to us," he said again, and stopped. "You want to believe in Rummage. She has been good to you, I own, but Caleb is a child. Even if they catch a slipstream, it's not likely that he'll know the Northern Dark for what it is. Ships that miss the exit are never seen again."

"What do you want me to do, Lake?" She folded her arms. "Do you want me to run to the barracks and petition their general on behalf of a brimstone beast, an off-world fraud, and her weird kid?"

A train whistle drifted through the lightless

air, oily and slick. Oliver yawned. "Very well. I do love a bad idea." He slid face-up into the dry washtub, arms and legs sprawled against the broken tiles. "Give me one hour. I haven't had a good nap since Brighton."

Ava sat with him under the beryl window. She sang a little, pale refrains about wind maidens who crouched in chimneys, and an angler with a voice so sweet that her boat floated by on spellbound shoals.

Her mother had always sniffed at the mention of music. "A waste of time," she said. "Ballads and books—what sort of wealth does that get you but imaginary coins?"

When Oliver started to snore, she spun the lock on her safe, gathered fistfuls of bright yellow bills, and let herself out into the hall.

Near the kitchen stood the untuned harpsichord. Its metal stand cradled books of sheet music—eastern shanties, lullabies, songs about red-haired witches stirring fires in the deep woods. They were tales that she loved, whose harmonies leaked into her dreams when the midsummer heat split the shroud of her sleep.

The scent of leather and mothballs rose from the bench when she lifted its lid. A stack of envelopes lay in the hollow, cinched together with a piece of twine. It was three weeks until Deliverance Eve.

Many winters ago, her father had thrown open their balcony doors and swung her skywards, chuckling as she reached for the strands of geese that tumbled south.

"When you are older," he said, "I will take you west with the paper shipment. You can see them along the meridian—tens of thousands, all calling to each other so they don't get lost."

Downstairs, traffic hummed. Ava blinked, and the envelopes turned cloudy and soft. Perhaps these were overtures of forgiveness. She imagined George Sandrino, settling into his study at the end of each day and reading aloud from the big almanac with no one to hear. When she was small, she had pictured his words as dancers, waltzing against the ornate notes of the latest opera house record.

Ava let the lid fall shut. In the drawing room, the deer-bone clock struck one. Caleb watched her from the loveseat. His eyes glowed, full and bottomless beneath the quick, white flash of a lighthouse.

"You don't look like a geomancer," she whispered. He put his thumb in his mouth and made no sound.

Ava crept into the kitchen and boiled coffee in a tarnished pot. She made a paste of honey and sumac to hide her bruise, sat on the counter and watched the blue-veined ivy sway. *You can do as you please*, she had told Sariel, before he was consumed by the nimbus of her desire. She was not sure that he would have pleased, had they been free of Ezra and the Empire. The thought disturbed her.

At half past one, Oliver Lake shambled in the hall. He tried to put his hands in his pockets, only to find that his jacket was on inside-out. "Cheers, darling," he said when she handed him her mug. "I must speak to Mrs. Sullivan before we leave."

Her toe snagged the stained dishcloth. He leaned towards her. She felt the ghost of his beard before it touched her skin.

"We would have made great lovers, you and I," he said, grinning with all his crooked teeth.

"I'm not your sort, Ollie," said Ava.

"And I'm not yours." He laughed and kissed her chin. "Maybe next life, if you believe in that sort of thing."

\* \* \*

Above the glass umbrella stand, a narrow square had been hacked into the ceiling. It was covered with wood whose planks bore fingers of mold, bent by the passage of autumn and spring. Oliver studied it without a word. When he was finished, he turned to Inday, who stood with her back to the open window. The fog gathered in crowns above her head.

"Make sure you're warm, Mrs. Sullivan," he said. "Your boy, too. It's a long way to the southern pier." He paused and murmured something, long and low in English. Whatever it was made the fortune-teller scowl.

Ava pulled a silver greatcoat from her closet and gave it to Inday, who made a show of brushing it off. She buttoned herself up to the throat and straightened the heavy collar.

"I don't have anything for kids," said Ava, running her palms along the edge of a broken top shelf. "I suppose these will have to do."

Together, they draped Caleb in a pair of thick cashmere scarves, tucking the trailing ends into his trousers and sleeves. He peered at them over a lump of knitted wool.

"Excellent." Oliver wrung his hands, set one

foot against the bar of a wall-bound ladder, and hoisted himself up. Tendons strained in his neck. He pushed at the planks until they splintered and snapped. Their screws came loose with a terrible crack. Above them, wind hissed. The darkness stood ready and open.

Ava turned to Inday, who gazed open-mouthed at the plaster-edged square. "That tunnel ends on the western landing," she said. "The exit door is supposed to be locked, but it never is. Must not keep the thieves from their houses."

"Are you certain?" Inday squinted. "How do you know this?"

Ava felt her face grow warm. "The woman they hired to fix the pipes last year," she said. "I was friends with her."

"Ah, Talia." Oliver chortled. His voice echoed against the rusty lengths of metal as he hauled himself into the crawlspace. "I had a feeling about that one. She disappeared with your fancy pocket watch that night you got fall-down drunk—and I told you she would. Deliverance Eve, was it?"

Ava glared at the soles of his shoes. "Lake," she growled. "Do you want every officer along the Climbing Sea to hear you?"

"Love hurts, Sandrino. It's a universal truth."

She hurled a clump of plaster at his disappearing boots. "There are no guards stationed at the black pier," she said, without looking at Inday. "It's a junkyard. I know someone who has a boat that will sail straight towards the Northern Dark, but if we don't show by half-past three, run. You can catch the sunrise barge. My money will take you all the way to Tesalonica. Captain Shaw can't touch you there; the Ash-and-Bone Queen does not bow to the House of Tong. Keep my revolver close. If you manage to find a slipstream, you can surrender yourselves at a waystation along the coast."

*Surrender yourselves to Joseph Henry Sullivan*, her mind whispered, traitorously. *Lake might not be there to save you.*

"Right." Oliver, turned onto his belly and stuck his arms through the gap. "Give him here."

Inday pressed her lips to Caleb's cheek. Then, she raised him high, bracelets jangling.

"Ma," the boy said. The word was an exhale, hardly a sound as he was hauled between sheets of dust. It was the first time that Ava had heard him speak. They clambered into the cobwebbed gloom. *Geese*, she thought, as the bald light of the flat trickled out. *Calling to each other so we don't get lost.*

In her pocket, the archer's knot sat like lead. The new world, she thought, contained no door that would bend to her key.

The ancient pipes rattled, ferrying wastewater and steam in shaky countercurrents. Ava felt the steel grow warm under her skin. From the flats below, the sounds of living rose: glass breaking, a chorus of howling kettles, the grunt and sigh of orgasm. When the metal cooled, the third-floor drunk burst into a fit of wracking sobs. At the head of their line, Caleb froze.

"It's all right, kid," said Oliver. "Some people can't handle their whiskey, is all."

The child remained where he was. Inday's voice snaked like a whip over Ava's shoulders. "Pagdali sa," she snapped. "If you do not move, I will leave you here!"

Gingerly, Oliver nudged Caleb. "Listen to your mother," he said.

Trembling, Caleb slid under an iron cross-beam and stumbled down a flight of stairs. Out they went, over wooden slats that shook at the joints, onto a landing glazed with rat dung. Ava turned the handle of a thick steel door. When it opened, she held her breath, waiting for the glint of armor and the thump of boots. There was nothing—only the high black cliffs and the sea, spitting its dregs at a strand of shoreline. Below them, New Dera was riotous with light and sound.

"This is the sluice." The rain had turned to eddies of snow. Inday looked accusingly at her. Coarse strands of hair streamed across her nose and mouth. "You took us by the wrong staircase."

"Patience is wealth." Where the ground was wet with foam, Ava knelt, climbing into a gully that fronted the waves. "Ezra forgets that our water mills are dry. All the sluices are dammed." Dirt crumbled under her hand till her fist struck metal. A bent gate stood, half-raised over a bed of sand. She waited while the others slid into the ditch behind her.

In the hollow, the bloated shadows of moths skittered over a screen of lamplight. The tunnel glowed, bright with the leavings of summer eels and their bioluminescent ooze. Ava pointed along a ribbon of stone. "Walk until you see the hawthorn roots. You'll come out in the Old Quarter. No hide-behinds, no knights." She smiled wryly. "People are rich there. Lots of churches and cradle money."

Inday was silent. The hard lines that streaked her face softened. She twisted the tail-eating serpent off her thumb and pressed it into Ava's open hand. "Lake tells me the Eighth Pike is hungry for children, like the barracks that bought you."

Ava blinked. "Mrs. Sullivan," she said.

"At the port of the Northern Dark, they will greet me with chains and a noose, and Caleb will be alone." Her eyes shone. She jerked her head at the silver ring. "It is only a trinket, but the dragon is good luck. He will keep you safe in the dark."

"We aren't at the Northern Dark yet."

"And what is that supposed to mean?" Inday opened her coat, pressing Caleb against her pleated skirt. Ava watched them go, pebbles on a tide that made them silent and small.

"Come." Her lungs felt like floes of pack ice. She turned to Oliver, who stood with his hands on the hilt of some invisible sword. "One hour running."

North of the sluice gate, the tunnel split in two. They came up through a wall that towered over Aurumine Street. It was the eve before the fast. Pale lanterns carved circles of light around taverns that strained with laughter and song. Between clouds of opium and pools of vomit, revelers swayed, dressed in bone masks and rose-thorn caps.

"Ollie," called Ava, voice lost under the noise of bells. "I should speak to Madame Rummage alone. She's not fond of strangers."

"Strangers." His breath warmed her neck. "The fine lady knows who I am."

"She knows about the drinks that you don't pay for." Ava sidestepped a girl who squatted at the mouth of a gorse-flaked bridge, lifting her skirts to piss into a shallow runnel. "You should have gone ahead with them. You still can."

Oliver put a cigarette between his lips. He snapped his fingers, and the unlit end began to smolder. "Listen to me." A firecracker burst. Its white trail moved like paint across his pointed cheeks. "You and I need to stay together."

"Why?" The bridge ended at an avenue crammed with winter foxglove and gambling dens. She helped herself to his cigarette, stubbing it out against the broken stones of a vacant warehouse. "You had no qualms about sending Inday off on her own."

"Inday is a quack with a crystal ball and a tender heart. They don't know that her boy is a geomancer—not yet—and it's you that Captain Shaw wants." He paused. "Well, us, I suppose—but he hates you."

"Why, thank you, Lake."

"Ava." Oliver faced her, tramping sideways down the street. "They will come for you first." He showed her his empty hands. "I'm a good marksman. My handler has fettered me, but if something goes wrong, I can still buy you time and miles."

She stopped in front of a teahouse. Dice rattled. A cavalcade of silhouettes spun against the makeshift door. "You can leave, too," she said. "Disappear between worlds. Geomancers are good at that."

Beneath the arch of Saint Genesius, the stone wolf kept watch, torchlight molten in her weathered grooves. A grin split his face. "Darling." He gave her a half-bow. "No matter what I do, I am well and truly fucked."

At the glyph-pierced portal, the rifles of guards in dove-grey masks rose between a smoggy river of carts and automobiles. Men called after her, leering and whistling as she went. Their ranks were scoured by brokers with knives, in search of those who had earned the wrath of the Paper House Queen.

Ava squeezed through a knot of women draped in silks. She pushed past arms and legs that staggered under the burden of too much wine, until the mob became a queue that ended at the gate, and the tall, thin man who kept it. She came to him, arms open and fond, and folded a bank note into his pocket. "For your trouble, Marcus." Her nose brushed his ear.

"Ms. Sandrino," he said. His eyes narrowed when they landed on Oliver Lake. "Not him. This one's tab is longer than a horse's cock."

"We're here to settle." She put a hand on Oliver's chest and willed him, furiously, to stay quiet.

"Girls don't pay for their lovers. Not even drinks." Marcus shook his head. "Paper House rules."

"Marcus. We were lovers, too." She laughed and canted her hips at him, turning through a quickstep that was all the rage in the capital. She thought of wine and August, and the sugar-apple grit between her teeth as she lay naked and flushed across his lap. Her fingers reached up and tightened the strings that held his mask. "I seem to remember paying for your share of drinks. Besides, when has Rummage ever been cross with me?"

Inch by inch, she felt the stone roll out of place. A sly satisfaction filled her when, beneath the puckered cotton, his mouth became a smile. "Ms. Sandrino," he said. The gate swung open. She kissed him quickly and hurried past.

The Paper Houses loomed over sepia taverns and nylon-trimmed eaves. Once, they were little more than sticks and pith. Now, they billowed like poisonous mushrooms, bellies swollen and red in the glow of the witch lights. Their sides shone with resin that drained from the roots of the Sleeping Land.

Ava turned west towards the highest tent, scrambling up the granite-and-seashell stairs with Oliver in tow. New Dera receded beneath them. Ahead was the black pier, tumbling like lace into a midnight sea. The scent of cooking oil trickled out from under the weighted canvas.

"Behave," she hissed, pulling back the stout brocade. "Rummage is an old lady. She doesn't want to hear your stories about Germanian chastity belts."

The atrium billowed with opium. A trio of parrots chuckled and groaned atop a heartwood stand, its metal crossbars white with droppings. Under an embroidered awning, a woman sat in a high-backed chair, watching them indolently from above her unlit cigarillo. "Good evening, Ava Sandrino," she said.

"Paz." Ava started. "You're alone. Where is Sophie?"

Around the legs of the chair, a coral python furrowed and stretched, big with the contents of its recent meal. "Madame Rummage's new pet," said Paz. "It seems the brothel has acquired a menagerie." She stood up, mindful of the serpent, and plucked a short sword from where it leaned against an empty cage. "Sophie's mother is ill—water in the lungs. I heard from Giles that she might not last the month."

"I'm sorry. Sophie is a sweet girl." Ava took off her coat and shoes and handed them to Paz.

"Death and taxes, my dear. Is that not what they say south of Blackwater?" Paz sheathed her sword and got to work, running her hands over the leather soles and combing through each crease and pocket. When she was done, she crooked a finger at Oliver. "You too, My Lord."

"Why?" Oliver folded his arms. "You hardly blink when I come through."

"You never bring anything," said Paz. "Not even money."

In the narrow silence, the games room hummed behind a bolt of elk hide. The bright notes of a mandolin drifted overhead, accompanied by laughter and the clink of glass. Oliver gave her a brittle smile and reached into his houndstooth jacket.

*Pieces of eight*, croaked one of the parrots, watching him expectantly.

"Get fucked, you chicken in silk clothes." A small handgun, a switchblade, and two throwing knives appeared. "Careful," he said, adding the last knife to the pile on the floor. "That one's covered in aether."

Delicately, Paz freed a pair of gloves from the sash around her waist. "The snuffbox, too," she said, sliding them on before emptying the gun and gathering the weapons from the floor. "I saw it when you unzipped your coat."

"It's tobacco," snapped Oliver.

"It's never tobacco," said Paz. "Even if it was, Madame Rummage does not permit her clients to carry their evils about. Anything you might want, you can purchase in here."

Grimly, Oliver handed her the ornate snuffbox. Paz arranged everything onto a shelf carved with the head of a lion and the tail of a fish. "Welcome to the Queen's Tent." She pulled a yellow kerchief from a bottom cubby and wrapped the bullets snugly inside. "You can pick up your things on the way out."

"I'll take my clothes now," said Ava. "I'm not here for work tonight."

"Is that so? What a miracle to behold." From the games room, a shower of sparks and laughter erupted. Paz grinned, holding out the rainproof coat and shoes. "Master Lake, you are in the company of one of Madame Rummage's darlings: the little songstress who can get anyone to sing. Oh, don't look at me like that, Sandrino. The old bird would sell her mother for a house on the coast, but she does have her favorites."

"Too kind, Paz." Quickly, Ava did up her buttons. The last one came loose in her hand. "Give my regards to Ismail and the girls," she said. "Perhaps I'll see them on Deliverance Eve."

The python lifted its head, tasting the air as Paz walked by. She tugged on a short silver chain, and the elk skin lifted.

*Open sesame*, screamed the parrots, one after another. Light and the throttled mass of voices toppled into the foyer. Ava rolled her hair between her fingers, tugging and twisting until it sat in an even knot. "Come," she said, catching Oliver by the thumb.

The crowds were thin tonight. Between the latticed arches of the games room, a black tree bloomed. Its branches and scarlet leaves pushed skywards, disappearing into the boards that concealed the upper level and jutting out into the snowy eve.

"Harpy wood," Madame Rummage had told her. "An evergreen plant that grows nowhere else. It was the first tree to sprout on New Dera. The Craftsman has blessed it."

The smell of perfume and lye stuck in her throat. Ava was certain that Madame Rummage did not believe any of it herself, and that the tree was just a tree, but the Paper House Queen was forever starved for coins. Hundreds of pounds of harpy wood were bottled and sold each week. The plant was an anathema against the scarring sickness. Its broth opened wombs, stopped up tears, and turned bedroom performances into fuel for myths.

"Snake oil," she had warned Oliver, when his eyes flitted wonderingly over the vials.

They picked their way down the terraced floor, through rows of people sitting shoulder-to-shoulder upon satin cushions, sharing sooty water pipes and ash-dotted tables. Women dressed in silk turned card tricks and read fortunes that were unfailingly promising. A young man and a dark-haired waif argued about politics on Chainlight Reef—*annexation to the Agia Marina is fair; Chainlight is hardly a country!*—faces flushed, pressed close to each other over a carafe of yellow wine.

In the rose quartz aisles, masked brokers prowled. Their white veils billowed like castaway phantoms. They removed empty bottles, refilled jugs of liquor and tea, and when they were signaled, left wordlessly at the heels of patrons and paper house girls. Negotiations were held near the larders, at long tables removed from the film of opium.

On the curved dais at the foot of the great tree, the drums and cymbals clashed. Firelight roared in a pit that yawed between theatres and dressing rooms. She had danced here before, draped in cotton scarves beneath the gaze of dockhands who tossed coins and shouted that they had been to this port and that along the Orchid Coast. When her tongue learned stranger, sweeter songs, she danced again, this time in sea silks gifted to her by wealthy diplomats and crooked priests.

Ava thought of the nook she had earned: a fur-trimmed seat and oakwood vanity high in the rafters of the Queen's Tent. Her bright scarves, she knew, would go to whichever girl they fit. The box of rouge and kohl would be discarded, and her songbooks would end their days in the musty closet of the arthritic dance master. The thought of her possessions scattered like carrion left a sour taste in its wake.

The electric lights flickered and dimmed. From among the clawed roots, a tall, sinewy woman rose, naked but for the steel chains and copper padlocks that gilded her body. The antique stage creaked under her toes. She caught Ava's eye and winked.

Saida was a contortionist from Upper Kestel. They drank together after work on black moon nights, sharing men, profits, and bottles of spiced rum. Ava recalled the wiry northerner leering at her over the rim of a wooden cup.

"I've been doing it since I was eight," Saida said, pulling her fingers in and out of joint. She spoke to Ava in the tongue that yoked the roads of their motherlands. "It doesn't hurt."

Still, the sight made Ava shiver. She forbade Saida from such demonstrations whenever they slept together, in rented quarters that smelled of pine sap and kelp. The contortionist would laugh. Everything was a game to her, so Ava kept her secret to herself: that these were among the fistful of nights she fell asleep without Ezra Shaw and the Orchid Coast lodged in her chest, iron-dark and heavy.

She took Oliver by the hand as the drums fell silent and Saida bent at the waist, limbs twitching against the burnished glow. They crowded into the stairwell, clambering up the wooden slats that drifted in midair around the gnarled trunk. Behind her, Oliver stumbled.

"A word for your boss," he said. "These stairs can't agree with the drunks."

"They don't." The block beneath her foot shuddered at the rude noise of bells. "She had an alchemist install them last week. Says they add to the ambiance of the place."

Someone shouted for whiskey. Ava stole a glance through the dark boughs and blood-bright leaves just in time to see the chains writhe across Saida's umber skin, the swell of bone as her shoulder left its socket. She freed herself from the steel that hugged her ribs. A round of applause went up. They cleared the landing, vanishing into a corridor lined with rented rooms.

In a crevice garlanded with black flowers, a storehouse stood open. An Ishenki girl knelt upon a crate, woven headdress pinched between her broken nails. Her purple smock was smudged with dirt. An enforcer with a scarred jaw towered over her, grey mask pulled down around his throat.

"You put your mark on our contract," he said. "I can't have you running off every time some broker shorts you—it's next to breathing for them, sweetheart! If this happens again, you will be shot."

"Then shoot me." The girl looked up. Her

eyes glowed, lambent as plastic buttons and surly over a bruised lip. "My brother lives by the graving dock," she said. "His wagons leave for Thrace tomorrow. Madame Rummage told us family visits are allowed."

"Only for those who intend to return." Gently, the enforcer put out his gloved hand. "Come now, peel off that getup. She wants you in chiffon and gold."

Ava watched as they disappeared down the floating steps. His rifle loomed like a sentinel. Their shadows left uneasy stains in the corner of her eye.

As they moved through the hall, the click of her heels pierced the winding sheet of murmured words and stifled cries. Stale sweat limned the air. It clung despite the kits of cinnamon and sandalwood the chambermaids burned at dawn. The hall became a ramp, then a loft flanked by six blackwood doors, polished and carved with the wings and horns of spotted deer.

Oliver let out a low whistle. "So," he said, "this is what you've been hiding."

"These rooms are for people like our Sambrese governor." Ava bent under a plaster frieze. "He stayed for two weeks, first with me, then with a pain-giver from Thrace. The man was stupid with opium and wormwood. He will owe the tent a favor soon—wait and see."

Chains of gargoyles watched from a granite perch. Their gaping jaws held back plague demons and earthbound spirits. Red ants crawled over half-eaten bowls of dates, left to molder until they were found by the morning brooms.

Years ago, the rough skirl of this place had frightened her. Now, it fit like a second skin. Each caller left behind bits of jetsam from their lives. She glimpsed it often between breaths, on the smell of their clothes, in all the things they said and did not say. Here, their disordered thoughts were taken apart and reordered, sewn into the pitted walls and mattress seams that would remember and be silent.

The final staircase curled towards the highest floor, where the offices of the bookkeeper and head enforcer stood locked and barred. Only the study glowed, lively with heat and the snap of a vinyl record.

"Madame Rummage," she called. "It's Ava. Is the cat tethered?"

No answer came, only the sob of a violin and the drone of someone humming along.

"Madame Rummage," Ava called again, waspish this time. "I've got company. If that wretched mouser bites, I won't think twice about kicking it in the face."

The humming stopped. Leather creaked. The vinyl record made a crumpling noise. "Plato is old, Ava Sandrino," said a voice from above. "It has been eight years since the incident. Would you kick an old man?"

Ava huffed and bounded up the last six steps. She peered around the doorframe before letting herself into the too-warm study.

Madame Rummage was smoking behind her cast iron desk, a fat blue caracal at her feet. The animal rolled over on the terracotta rug.

"I saw your latest import downstairs," said Ava. "Are you opening a zoo, now?" She clicked her tongue nervously at Plato, who lashed his tail and spat. He had left his mark on her heel many winters ago. She had never forgiven him.

Madame Rummage grunted. She set her pipe down upon its well-worn stand and glanced at them, lips parted over needle-sharp teeth. "The snake is bound for Lithra," she said. "So are the birds. A young man in Karnak is paying half a million lira to have them housed here." Her white eyelashes flickered. The smallest gleam of displeasure crossed the sharp bones of her face. She plucked three crystal tumblers from under her desk and filled them with gin from an unmarked jar. "Oliver Lake, the marksman. An honor." She raised her glass against the quaking hearth light. "The Guild has their war machine up and running, I hear. Your mother has done great things for them—feats of science that even your military was unable to accomplish with more funding and fewer critics."

"The Guild has many war machines," said Oliver, carefully.

"But none like this." Madame Rummage squinted. "An alloy of brimstone and witch gold. A marvel of engineering. The One O'clock King is red with envy." She waved her tumbler until the blue gin kissed its lip. "Please, be seated."

"Ava." Oliver beamed. "You never told me that Her Majesty is a bird woman." He settled himself deep into an overstuffed chair. "I spent eight months with your people in the ice fields. Modern navigation can never repay you."

"And neither can you, according to our records." Her mouth puckered. "Those are not my people," she said. "I was born in the inter-world markets, to a whore who died when the scarring sickness filled up her lungs with blood. I do not know these ice fields you speak of."

Without blinking, Oliver lifted his drink and

drained it. "A black-market daughter," he said. "Even better."

The Paper House Queen laughed. The sound was rheumy and soft. "Your friend owes me more money than the treasury of this wretched city, but I might be willing to forgive the debt." She gestured at the empty seat beside her. Ava slid into its velvet arms, swishing the gin around in its glinting vessel while she watched the rise and fall of Plato's ribs. Above them, vast wall hangings trembled at the bark of drums. They were painted with strange characters, red handprints pointing the way along a network of unknown roads.

Madame Rummage's blue-grey skin ran with firelight as she bent over her desk, sifting through the pile of ledgers. She came up with a thin piece of paper and waved it triumphantly in the air. "This is called a *check*, Ava Sandrino," she said. Dark venom moved in storms under her nails. "I have been trying to convince you of its worth for months. Open a bank account like respectable people."

"I'm not here to discuss payments," said Ava. She glanced at the grandfather clock that stood beside an open window, its black hands stark against a lavender face. Half an hour, she thought, and swallowed her words. After eight years, she had earned the right to say almost anything that she pleased, but the queen would not be rushed inside her own castle.

Madame Rummage sighed, running a narrow hand down the front of her pearled gown. "I do not know how you get people to speak to you." Her short crest of feathers rattled when she nodded. "That is one piece of performance art I have never been able to figure out. A fine singer, yes, but no siren. I certainly would not drown for you." She took a sip of her drink and refilled Oliver's glass. "Anyway, aren't you supposed to be on holiday? Ester Blanchard from accounting says you bought a ticket to Sun Tooth Isle."

Ava shifted. A tightness throbbed above the bridge of her nose. "I don't think I'll be going on holiday anytime soon." There was nothing for it. "Forgive me, Mother," she said. "I came here to ask a favor."

"You have not called me *mother* since your twentieth birthday. That was an affair to remember. I thought you would sweat liquor until the end of autumn." Madame Rummage clinked her glass against Oliver's and drained them both. She closed the ledger and shut her eyes. "I know what you are here for. They have that wraith hanging in a birdcage over the water. You want to send him through the Northern Dark, and now, being a fugitive, you will want to go with him." She opened her eyes. "Ms. Sandrino knows that I have access to unmarked boats. She has come to beg."

For a long time, the only sounds were the heartbeat of the clock, the pounding of the drums against the floor, and the pull and rasp of air in Plato's lungs.

She almost denied it. Ava was a keeper of secrets, not a fount. But the clock chimed, and her thoughts of blackmail faded. She was a wooden pawn, and Madame Rummage moved her as she pleased. She drained her glass and said, voice heavy, "Can you help us?"

"This is quite the disaster." Rummage stood, tugging idly at the wall hangings and leaning down to inspect a big teal globe. Plato crawled after her, belly dragging. She spun the globe. It turned on its bronze axis, coming to rest upon the Landless Kingdoms, the narrow ridge that poured burning soil into the highest ocean. "I am always able to help. You know this. But I need you to do something for me in return."

"Madame Rummage," growled Ava. "I am not in a position to lend anyone favors right now."

"Nor are you in a position to take that tone with me." The bird-woman scratched Plato behind the tufts of his long, grey ears. "Ezra Shaw is angrier than a peacock in rut."

Ava stared at the bottom of her glass. She felt nineteen again, weeping in front of the metal desk the night the barracks had turned her out. "He doesn't have warrants yet," she said. "It's been less than a day."

"From fury comes ingenuity," said Madame Rummage. "Your Captain Shaw is impatient. He could not wait twenty-four hours for three arrest warrants. Forget the House of Tong. He has gone to the Pit Lords." She ambled over to the open door and gazed into the hall. Her head snapped towards Oliver Lake. "You know who the Pit Lords are, don't you, boy?"

From the corner of her eye, Ava saw that Oliver's hands were motionless in his lap. "Everybody does," he said. "Black market royalty, some of them geomancers."

"Precisely. They will welcome you to rot in an off-world prison, and fabricate your crimes against the One O'clock King. It will look like extradition. Ezra Shaw will not be punished for acting out of turn. He does not care about trials or jails or justice. He wants to hurt you, is all." Madame Rummage took her pipe from its stand and tapped its ashes into the fireplace.

Her shoulders cracked when she straightened. "He figured that you would come. His squire paid me twenty-thousand lira so they could park their hounds outside. One of my brokers is tipping him off right now."

Ava bolted from her seat. "Get your things, Lake," she said. "We have to leave."

Plato lurched upright, snarling. The dark points of his ears stood like daggers.

"Hold on." Madame Rummage seized the caracal by his thick red collar. "You have been good for the Paper Houses, Ava. You have done things for me that are above and beyond what is required of a pleasure girl. I would not throw you to the dogs."

"Is that what this is?" Ava leaned against the turntable, tightening the straps of her shoes. "Gratitude?"

Madame Rummage bowed her head. "They will be here in less than five minutes," she said. "The room closest to mine is empty and unlocked. It has a staircase that leads into the kitchens and out."

"I trusted you." The words left Ava in a strangled wheeze. "I knew you were greedy, all right—selling lies in Karnak and drugs to junkies—but you said—" her tongue stumbled, growing simple and coarse. "I thought you took care of your own." *Not like the Knighthood. Not like Demetra Sandrino.*

"And I am taking care of you, am I not?" Madame Rummage raised her eyebrows. The scales on her neck were black in the licking flames.

"I'm not one of your whippets." Rage lit Ava's skin like a brand. "That's what you think we are, isn't it? You throw money into baskets and watch us run."

"And you are the fastest I have." Step by step, Madame Rummage closed the gap between them. "I know you," she said, "every single one, down to the scullery maid with no right foot." Ava forced herself not to flinch at the sight of the needle teeth, the purple poison that lay coiled beneath her tongue. "Your interests are mine, even when it puts me out of pocket. Did I not forgive the advances you took when you could not afford your bangles and silks? Who do you think put Sophie's mother in hospice? The girl is easily replaced. I could have rid myself of her and hired a new attendant the second she sailed for Thrace. Do not forget who I am."

"Thank you, Mother," said Ava. "I'll think of you in front of Captain Shaw's firing squad."

The silence stretched and twisted like a harp string being tuned. Madame Rummage snorted. "Always so dramatic," she said. She knelt, sliding her fingers under and around Plato's collar. Something clinked. She tugged it loose and held it out. It was a metal square, pressed with the head of a blue ibis. "Well? Are you going to listen to me, or not?"

"Ava." Behind her, Oliver rose. "I think—"

"Make it quick." She snatched up the token and crammed it into the coin purse that sat in her pocket. The bird woman gestured. Grudgingly, Ava helped her to her feet.

"People believe that slipstreams dissolve at the highest tropic," Madame Rummage began, "but they are the skeleton of this world. I have a boat ready to go. You will sail to the edge of the Northern Dark with half a ton of al-Sarif brimstone. A captain in the house of Lady Ink has paid its ransom in gold."

"Lady Ink is a Pit Lord." Ava felt the blood leave her face. "Exporting brimstone to a black-market servant means the firing squad. No trial, no barrister."

"The Empire and the Guild have had their monopoly for long enough. One cannot buy black market goods and starve black market interests. I would not have told you, Daughter, but your wraith would have smelled it the second he set foot on the vessel." She nodded at Oliver, eyes like melted bronze. "My boat will go only so far, of course. I need a geomancer who can steer her into the mouth of the Northern Dark. There will be river ghosts, too." Her long teeth flashed. "You will keep the greedy tarts off our cargo. They do love all that shines."

"The black-market cities have been at our technology for decades." Oliver shook his head, lips pulled into a disbelieving half-smile. "They know what we're doing with brimstone alloys. I'd be a traitor."

"You're already a traitor," said Madame Rummage. "Why not make yourself useful? Be of assistance to an old woman such as myself." She turned to Ava. "The guards at the holding cells belong mostly to me. The Empire pays their stipends, but they have been living large on Paper House money for years. Some of them are knights, some are geomancers, and some are sell-swords from Sturling-on-Rhone. If you make it there within the next fifteen minutes, a lieutenant named Sithera Nighpiper will be waiting with a boat. Give her that token. She will know what it means."

"And what does it mean?" Ava shook her coin purse at the Paper House Queen. "Another call for my arrest, this time from you?"

"The tongue in your head, child," she hissed. "Drop anchor at Blackwater and leave the vessel where it floats. The place is a marsh, almost five-hundred leagues from the nearest city, with no paths into the otherworlds but the Northern Dark. No one will search you. I made sure of that." She paused. Regret filled the lines of her brow. "They have something special for you, boy. The Pit Lords have sent a geomancer. I think you have met before. She is a prizefighter from a fishing village who has caught the eye of the One O'clock King. This time, your handler will look the other way."

"No," said Oliver. "The Shaw family is rich, but they have no connections, not even to the House of Tong. How did Ezra bend the ear of the Pit Lords? There are rules."

"Yes, Master Lake, but there is also unrest, and that does not bode well for our economies. Treaties must be honored so that money and goods can flow." She pulled a terrycloth mouse from her sleeve and tossed it at Plato. The cat stared at it, unmoved. "The local governments are tired of guild interference—geomancers like you, sticking their heads into property spats and philosophizing over the personhood of wraiths. A statement must be made. Breaking your bones is not enough. They will want you denatured."

Oliver blanched. "Denaturing is for war criminals."

"Times are changing." She poked the mouse with her toe. "Now, the fact remains that you are a Lake. Your mother is a Barrowcrown. No Eighth Pike marksman would dare bring you in, but a mercenary geomancer might. Who would care? She is not known to them. There would be no rescue. In all the chasms and ravines in the lands of the One O'clock King, you would never be found."

"There are always rumors in the stables and barracks." His voice flickered like the coastline on a still, hot day. "Where did you hear this one?"

Her lips thinned. "I am not of this world. I was sent here from the black-market cities. My ears and heart remain in the black-market cities. Leave the study door open," she said. "It must look like you heard them coming and ran."

"I will never forget this," said Ava.

"Give it a month." Coolly, Madame Rummage set her palm against an unlit lamp and pushed. Glass shattered when it hit the floor. "Over here," she shouted. "The bastards took off!"

Beneath them, the drums faltered and ceased. Someone screamed. Ava gripped Oliver by the sleeve. His face was the color of unlined paper. "This way," she said.

They fled the study. In the cobalt glow of the hall, Ava fumbled with the latch that held the next room shut. Somewhere in the dark, a hoarse curse echoed—*what is this*? Cotton sandals whispered under the noise of spurs. The lacquered wood grew damp with her sweat.

"Ava—hurry," said Oliver.

"I am." His fear turned her joints to water. Twelve yards away, the last landing creaked.

"Bring Seknat," a voice boomed. "We're not going after the Lake boy alone—I don't care if he's crippled. Tell her to take a light."

The latch lifted. Ava pushed at the door. It opened several inches, only to stop short when it thumped against what she thought was a dresser. She swore and drove her shoulder into the spongy balsa. Then, Oliver's arms curved over her head, and the door moved with a screech that seemed to fill the entire tent.

They squeezed through the gap, scaling wardrobes and chairs that had been left there in haste and forgotten. The space reeked of mangoes and kitchen fumes. Thin shelves groaned under the weight of dusty books, leather floggers, steel clamps and cartonnage masks painted with the grins of beasts.

"Christ. Twenty-thousand lira, and she can't afford proper storage?" Oliver clambered after her onto a canopied bed. When they disturbed the folded sheets, blue-green moths rose in pearly wisps from the covers.

"A man died in this room," Ava said. Her teeth chattered. The racket of their hunters as they cleared the landing made her jump. She stumbled towards the window, dark with the branches of a thin white tree that grew, untrimmed, against it. "Some merchant from Iberia. His heart gave out while he was getting the ride of his life on one of our girls. I heard he was nearly a hundred."

"The lecher." Oliver kicked aside a wheeled cart. Its silver frame crashed into an orange unicycle. "There are worse ways to go—this, for one, if we don't pick up our feet."

She heaved the window open to sound of boots flying up the corridor. "Stop," someone roared. "The House of Tong commands you!"

They tumbled into the snowy night, followed by the cry of splintering wood. The staircase beneath them had been enclosed once—a passage for servants between the rented rooms and kitchens. Now, it stood rusty and unused, the cloth awnings peeled back and sold during a lean year. Ava and Oliver took the steps three at a time, crushing ice and cigarette butts under their shoes until they reached the base of the tent, where the lamps of boats on the Climbing Sea flickered beneath the muted glow of oven fire.

At the end of a wooden strut swayed a tasseled rope, heavy with polished call bells. A handgun and three knives spun on its fraying knot. Oliver tore them free. He checked to see that the bullets were in the chamber and the blades undamaged before settling them back into his coat.

"Your guardswoman is something else," he said. Behind the purple canvas, shadows moved. The grind and ring of the kitchens went on.

"Paz." Ava felt like spitting. "She knew what was going to happen."

Overhead, the room flowered with light. Figures like stains in the glare streamed after them, the glint of steel leaping down from the sill.

"The bone fires," said Ava. "It's the fastest way to the pier."

They raced into the foothills that girded

the lesser tents. Between alleys shored up with limestone, carpets of rat bones and pomegranate husks appeared. The carcass of a white dog crowned the frozen square that marked the end of Highwater Place. She turned left, where the city cleaved into unnamed roads, jostling through crowds of people whose faces seemed to fade like ink in water. Her throat burned. There was a warm wetness in the curve of her shoe, where the skin of her big toe had split.

"Wait." Behind her, Oliver slowed. Ava whirled towards him. He looked sick and drawn, gasping in the yellow arc of a teahouse lantern. In the distance, the lighthouse loomed, and the steel cages hovered at the ends of massive chains kept afloat by a trick of off-world alchemy.

"Ollie." She exhaled waxen streams of clouds. "We can't stop here."

"The hide-behinds," he said. "If they decide to get brave, there's not a lot I can do. My boss has her claws in me." He struck his chest with a fist. "I can feel her here. The earth-lines are still in my hands, but moving them will be hard."

"The hide-behinds are afraid of light." She turned, heading down a street that squeezed into a byway lined with older stones. Sweat froze on her skin. "And I'm not afraid of them."

At first, the click of her shoes and the scratch of her breath were the only sounds that walked with her. Then, Oliver was at her heels. "Ava," he said. "It's not your fear they're after."

"Two city blocks." She paused in a gas-lit alley, tearing the shoes off her feet and tossing them into a pile of fishing wire. "That's how far the bone-fires are. Just two city blocks."

Brick by brick, the alley grew houses, and the houses became flats—high, narrow buildings with rotting walls and crumbling chimneys. Vagrants, unfit for the shelter of Saint Genesius, peered out at them, eyes filmy with opium or the ravages of the scarring sickness. One by one, they returned to what passed for sleep.

Somewhere unseen, the surf hummed and hawed. Ava stopped. Her naked toes prickled with cold. She pointed at a fork in the ribbon-thin street, where the ground was damp and yielding. "This way," she said. "This is west."

Where the lamps went dark, the driftwood houses began. They ran into each other, dappled braids of wood bent together and smeared with flame-snuffing pitch. She had walked this way once, in the grey light of dawn. When darkness fell, the enforcers closed off the roads that ran towards the bone-fires and the sea.

Above them, the lighthouse went about its endless sweep. Ragged pennants flew from fragmented rooftops, stitched with arms she did not recognize—a fiery spindle, a stylized frog whose wide mouth overflowed with petals and thorns. Piles of refuse studded the space between walls, and limestone fumes oozed through long seams in the earth, mingling with the dark effluence of coal. It would be days before the smell of wood smoke and burning trash left her hair.

Women in white scarves and pewter rings stared, clustered inside their circles of sandy forge light. They tended fire pits and cauldrons, speaking among themselves in the checkered words that bridged this world and the next. One of them broke from her group and turned to Ava as she passed. Beneath a champagne headdress, her hair was gathered in towering rings. Blue paint stained her lips.

"Hey there, mademoiselle," she said, in blurry French. "Are you here for an amulet? Or an iron poppet, maybe? My husband is at his forge. He is an Ishenki man—can bend metal like wool."

"No, thank you." Ava gave a watery smile. "We are just passing through."

A rush of laughter curled between the

women. "Nice place for a stroll," one of them called. The bray of their merriment hung and shimmered in coats of flame and heat.

When Ava was a Paper House novice, Madame Rummage had told her that the bone-fire denizens were a marriage of nomads from Chainlight Reef and exiles from across the Northern Dark.

"Their men are smiths," the Paper House Queen had said one night, over a meal of dried cherries and palm wine. "They stay awake in the dark, with all their fires ablaze. They think that light keeps the hide-behinds away. Everybody does. Then, when the sun rises—" she snapped her fingers. "Their doors are shut and their curtains are drawn. No one sees them. It does not work, of course. Not quite. The creatures have got in their skulls, but they are too mad to know it."

"Then what scares the hide-behinds?" Ava tilted her chin insolently at Madame Rummage. "Prayers to the Craftsman? Pennies for the saints?"

"Your health," said Madame Rummage, raising her glass. They toasted and drank, and spoke of other things until the sky grew light and the night trains went quiet.

Above the rustling of the forges came a concert of tankards and plates. Three children sat around a pot that simmered over an open pit. They peered out from under veils of fragrant steam: cumin and caraway, a young cow brined in lemon and sage. A blonde girl with one tooth waved at Ava, face framed by the thick steel handle.

Oliver laughed. It was a high, tight note that bounced along the lane and vanished. "They have a nursery rhyme up north," he said. "It's that bit about Silas Levenstein, who got lost looking for Blackwater and spent a night and two days battling the hide-behinds. He was a geomancer, you know. Built the biggest conflagration there ever was, from earth lines and driftwood and the bones of the dead. They still got him in the end. Catchy thing, that."

"Lake." The hairs on her arms stood up. "Now is not the time."

She felt the gaze of the watchers in white. The tale was old and worn: here, they were touched by some evil. The priests at Saint Genesius refused to assign them funeral plots within the city grounds. Their fires were fed with corpses instead of coal, to please the gods that walked on blood.

The sound of metal skittering across the soiled eaves made Ava freeze.

"Keep going." The hand that Oliver pressed between her shoulders trembled. "Don't look back, and don't look up."

On the charred ground that belted the fire pit, a dark-haired woman appeared and lifted the girl child onto her breast. "A hide-behind," she shrilled, fearful and rapt. "A hide-behind is on the street, folks! A hide-behind is on the street!"

A great murmur went up behind them, a susurrus of jewelry and cloth. From the corner of her eye, Ava saw a skull made of steel and bone, a gaping socket picked clean by time. It bounded across a threadbare awning and was gone.

"I said, don't look." Oliver's fingers were on her head, turning it towards the broken coast. "You can see the lighthouse steps from here. Keep your eyes down."

"Quit that." Ava swatted him away. "I can tell my own eyes what to do."

Only, she could not. As the crash of waves grew deep and clear, the soft, black spots at the edge of the forges waxed like moons. She glanced at them over the line of her wrinkled collar. In the darkness, something looked back. It walked parallel to her, crawling behind doorframes and squirming under lintels each time she caught its shape.

"The hangman's trees," she heard Oliver say. "Eight-hundred yards, tops."

Through the smog of the metropolis, a church bell clanged. An ache settled in her limbs. The lighthouse and its hanging cages were far away, monstrous and cold on their perch by the sea. The night-burning forges beckoned, thick with deathless fires and shifting coke hearts. Her legs floundered in front of a house that brimmed with fiddle song. Seated in front of the roaring blaze that spilled onto the wooden stoop was Sariel.

A dull happiness flooded her at the sight of him. He was wearing a white linen shirt and suspenders spun from cashmere. Everything gleamed, from the wine glass in his unscarred hand to the sable horns that rose from their mass of curls. When he stood, the driftwood protested, loud and alive.

"Ava," he said, in a voice that sounded like Ezra Shaw. "It is late. We should be going home."

"They are after me." Her words floated like spider silk between them. "I can't stop here."

*Ava*, somebody said, far in the distance.

With a wry smile, Sariel set the wine glass

down. Its base left dimples in the dirt. "They do not know we are here," he said. "Nobody does. Come. We will return to the flat, and you can go back to the Queen's Tent in the evening." He opened his arms, and she remembered suddenly the crude eagerness in his palms, the tremor of his hips between her legs.

"Sariel." The name was askew in her mouth. "You put a child in me. You're a fleshblood wraith. That's what everyone is saying."

He paused. Something moved behind his eyes; the sight of it made her think of lizards stalking mice in the window box.

*Ava!* Her name burst like light through a tube.

"I don't know you," she said. "I certainly don't love you. I liked Ezra Shaw the moment I saw him. I loved him after a year. Love takes time."

"You do not have to love me," he said. "Some things are greater than love. You know what I mean."

At her feet, strands of dwarf mallow sprouted, spotted with flowers the color of plums. The coal-fume night disappeared. Tall houses with scrolled roofs erupted from the driftwood walls. Sariel wore a cravat now, and nursed a blue china mug filled with tea. He stepped off the marble staircase and stood so close to her that steam from the vessel left her cheeks damp and flushed.

*Ava fucking Sandrino!* The tall houses shuddered. *Can you hear me? We have five minutes.*

"It was never love you were after." He bared his teeth. His canines glared with brass. "For nine long years, you have cultivated your wealth in the Paper Houses. If you leave now, what was it for? You will have to start again, among off-world strangers. Where will you end up? Maybe like Inday. A Blackwater Bride." He put the china mug in her hand. It did not burn. "In Babel, you would be a queen. Your mother would crawl to you on her knees, begging for a grain of your good fortune. Is that not what you want?"

"Yes," she whispered. Beneath her, the dwarf mallow tightened in thickets around her legs. "Sariel, it's not too late, is it? I can go back to Madame Rummage. I want to stay. If I leave—Oliver—she says that they'll denature him."

"Do you know what that means, Ava Sandrino?"

"No."

Sariel giggled like a pie dog at dusk. "A brutal practice. The geomancer that hunts him will tear the magic from his spine and leave him dumb and nerveless in the vault of the One O'clock King. Is that what you want for your friend?"

"No!" Ava recoiled. "Of course not."

"You are in over your head," said Sariel. "There has been trouble for three lifetimes already. Madame Rummage will protect you. She is more than able."

"She is a black-market daughter," murmured Ava. "She said so, herself. I'm tired of running. There is nowhere that I wish to go."

"Of course." His hands traced the line of her throat, flitting over her belly, swollen and full. "There is nowhere to go. Stay here with us. There will be brandy and music by the fire. Sing me your songs, the ones that you hear in your sleep."

"My summer songs." There were clouds in her eyes. "I never told you about those."

*Ava*, the voice said again. This time, it was close and bright.

The world fractured and shook. Sariel looked at her with empty eyes. His head tilted and he fell, coming apart in streams of coins and shards of blue china. She reeled back, heart thundering as the dwarf mallow receded and the bright houses turned to sand. The scent of wood smoke returned. Oliver Lake crushed her in a bruising embrace.

"Ollie." She gasped as they sprang apart. "Ollie—what was—"

"Hide-behind got you," he said, face white with pain. "I took it apart, but I won't be able to do that again. We have to go."

"That was a hide-behind?" Sprigs of hair stuck to her clammy cheeks.

"I told you, they don't want your fear." His arm swept the street, where dozens of eyes watched vacantly from half-open windows. "These fine folks say their forges and hearths keep them safe, but the visions are like opium. You will always be searching for things you cannot have. The creatures come back, night after night. They grow strong while your mind decays."

"Like wraiths." The words came without thought. Phantom vines curled around her knees. "They want the things our thoughts create."

"No." He shook his head. "Wraiths are filter feeders. These are parasites."

High above them, a steam clock howled. "Three minutes," she said.

They left behind the driftwood shacks, scuttling down a narrow lane that turned from dirt to gravel. Ava knew that the not-Sariel was something to be feared, but her spine was a compass needle, pulled back towards the stoop and the monster in fine clothes.

Up ahead, green petrels came to roost in the

cottonwood stands. The sepia glow of witch lights bathed rows of hothouse plants. Bunches of hollow squash dangled on twine, filled with unlit candles and rum-soaked cakes. These were prayers to Saint Genesius, and to the heathen Christ who ruled the world of Blackwater.

Ava ground her teeth against the numbness in her toes. Bits of rock made craters in her feet. Off-world, there would be a new Paper House Queen, and saints that went by foreign names. How much did infant clothes cost in the shops of the foreign townships?

At the crossroads, electric torches guttered. A thicket of hangman's trees rose in the freezing air. She saw their barren peaks, crooked like the beams of gallows. Their leaves and thorns shone like shields. They seemed welded together, locked with unsettling symmetry against anyone who might approach. The birdcages sailed above, dark thumbprints in an ocean that flowed between isles of stars.

"Ava." Oliver's voice left him in a wet rattle. "Not too close. The hangman's sap will melt your lungs." He pulled his shirt over his mouth and nose, waving into the October fog. "Guard," he called. "We're from the Queen's Tent! Is there a Sithera Nighpiper about?"

Behind a smokescreen of searchlights and snow, lumbering silhouettes plodded back and forth. One of them paused, half-hidden by the spine of a weathered guardhouse. Ava saw the blink of glass. A beaked mask and blue-green goggles took shape in the dark. "No further," said a woman, throaty and faint as radio static. "Did Ilsë send you?"

"Ilsë?" Oliver paused. His shoulders rose.

"Ilsë Rummage." Ava nodded until her curls came loose. "Yes, Ilsë sent us. Are you Sithera Nighpiper?"

The beaked mask drifted closer. "Do you have the seal?"

Ava tore the deer-skin purse from her pocket. She riffled through it, pushing her fingers past bronze coins and banknotes until the golden bezel of the token flickered in the muddy night. The head of an ibis peered up at her. Bits of blue wax dripped from its wattle.

"Here," she said. "All yours."

The beak bobbed and swayed. Beneath it was a body encased red plates of armor, and above it a crown of straw-yellow hair. A gloved hand plucked the signet like a winter berry; the other gripped a war hammer, its black head fuzzy with aether down. "Good," she said, rolling it over three times before tucking it into the joint between her sleeve and glove. "I am Sithera. You are very nearly late."

"Tea with the queen, darling," said Oliver. He removed his pocket square and motioned for Ava to cover her face with the striped green silk.

"I'm not your darling," said Sithera. "This brimstone business is bad, Lake. You should have listened to your handler. Now, stay put. The forest is opening." The war hammer came up under Oliver's nose. "If anything should happen, we do not know each other. That goes for both of you. My comrades will vouch for me before the Knighthood and the Guild."

"Understood." Oliver tried to grin, but his face dissolved into a white mask of pain. Ava thought of the water closet, and the bruises that sat like lightening under his skin.

"There is a blue ship anchored at the pier." Sithera jerked her thumb over her shoulder, towards the lighthouse on its crag. "Your Blackwater Bride and her son are waiting by the vessel. Oh, don't look surprised, Sandrino. Ilsë was a Pit Lord, and I don't think retirement suits her." A ball of pomander fell from the cloth and wire mask. She caught it before it hit the ground.

"Tell her to speak to him, then." Ava felt the

frost steal into her feet. "The One O'clock King. His people move against us, and we have done nothing to them."

"Nobody speaks to the One O'clock King," said Sithera. "Just Lord Silk, and he has given his ruling. Be grateful. The Paper House Queen is fond of you." She shoved the pomander back into the roof of her beak. "No time to waste. That boat is keyed to you. It will not raise anchor until you are on deck. If you don't show, they will sail for Tesalonica with the sunrise barge."

Mutely, Ava watched as Sithera stamped towards the guardhouse. "Hey," called Sithera. "Ilsë's people are here for the fleshblood wraith! Tell Salah to cut him down."

One of her companions handed her a dented mug. She filled it with coffee from a cauldron that boiled at the entrance, lifted her mask and took a sip. Above her, the hangman's trees shifted and groaned.

Thorn by thorn, the thicket opened with a flight of watery claps. Branches slid apart like cogs, and the blue-black heart of the brushwood pulsed. Ava craned her neck. The birdcages rocked, bound to the forest at the ends of vine-capped chains. One of them tilted and jerked.

Aether flared. A dozen guns were racked

in noisy disarray. The dark greenery knit itself shut, dragging the lonely cell earthwards. Buffeted by streams of icy wind, it came to rest with a clank and a thud. The metal bars were lost between the scarred arms of creepers and parasitic roots.

At the guardhouse, Sithera drained her cup and straightened her mask. Snow squelched under her boots. She stopped ten paces short of the birdcage, war hammer raised. "Wraith," she barked. "Exit."

Between the bars, there was a ripple of motion. The door creaked. Sariel stumbled out, still stripped to the waist.

"Sorry about the goods." Sithera held the war hammer steady as he passed. "He tried to run. It's nothing a good doctor can't fix."

"The trees," said Ava. The scent of bergamot on the pocket square plugged her lungs. "He's got no mask."

"He's a wraith. A dose that would kill us all might make him dizzy." Sithera lowered her war hammer. The beak swung towards them. "All right, you two. I've done my job. Come and get him."

Oliver pulled his shirt tight across his face. "Wait here," he said, and sprinted towards the birdcage. Sariel took two limping steps before his legs gave out. The geomancer caught him as he fell, wriggling out of his houndstooth jacket and draping it over the sagging shoulders. Together, they hobbled away from the tower and its cloudy brake of hangman's trees.

On wooden legs, Ava went to meet them. Her skin and eyes stung in the rain of killing sap. Then, her hands were filled with him: the torn skin that left comet tails of blood on her palms, the snow-stippled silk of his curls. From under Oliver's coat, he looked at her like a drowning man.

"We're leaving now," she said. "Into the Northern Dark." Her fingers skated across his swollen jaw while the vastness of the night and all the worlds it hid turned like carousels in her skull. "We can do whatever we please. We can go where we want."

"You would come with me," he croaked. His fingers were icy and rough. "You do not know me. Your work is here, and your books and your friends."

"Friend," said Oliver. "We don't get out much, me and her."

The lighthouse lamp went by, igniting the arc of Sariel's horns. "I come from nowhere," he said. "I might be going nowhere."

"Better move." Sithera dragged her mug against the empty cage. "Salah says there are knights on the ridge." She paused. "And a geomancer. That slipstream will close before dawn."

"You come from the fever ships." Ava fixed the collar of the jacket, doing up the buttons and rolling back the too-long sleeves. "And before that, the Landless Kingdoms. As for where we are going—" her throat closed. "People like us have nothing to explain, isn't that right, Ollie? Not even to ourselves."

"He's going have to run on it," said Oliver. He smoothed his shirt and tilted his chin at the leg that Sariel favored. "He's a wraith. He can stand it, can't you?"

Ava opened her mouth, horrified. She was about to remind him that, while earthworms could survive being chopped into bits, there was no reason to subject them to such an experience. A far-off whistling stopped her.

The guardhouse fell silent. A cloud of golden smoke tore the sky in half. It hung smoldering against the winter constellations, spilling over the wheels of steam-powered clocks and flooding the thousand rows of hangman's thorns. A bullet tore free from the miasma, thudding into the frosty earth. On the ridge above the cross-roads, a string of figures emerged.

"That was for you, Lake," someone cried. The words bounded from her, mirthful and deep. "Us geomancers have no business with single-world convicts. Give them up."

Oliver stood still as marble. His clothes and hair were drenched with sweat, eyes like copper in the guardhouse lights. He took the gun from his waistband and thrust it at Ava.

"You know how to use it," he said. "No more shortcuts. No more bone fires. It's a straight shot from here to the boat, and the poppy fields are open ground. You won't make it—not with me."

"Come on, Lake," said the woman on the ridge. The muzzle of a rifle protruded over her shoulder. "Even your dear, sweet mother knows you've been bad. I spoke to her myself. She says they'll get you for something—insubordination, manslaughter, conduct unbecoming a marksman. Why not aiding and abetting?" She laughed. The sound was honey in a firepot. "I will give you thirty seconds."

Oliver turned a violent red. "My mother would not wipe her hands on your clothes, you fishmonger bitch," he bellowed, loud enough to make Ava start. When he looked at her, the copper in his eyes had turned to hammered silver. The symbol for the magnetic north teetered and spun. "Take your wraith and go." He nudged her towards the western road. "The boat and slipstream will know who you are. Watch the skies. Look for a bay filled with great rings of stars. If you cannot find it and the water runs black, turn the rudder east by northeast. It will take you to Tesalonica."

"I've never sailed before," she said. "Inday doesn't seem like the nautical type, either."

"The ship will know its course. You only have to board, darling."

"Ollie." Freezing wind settled between her lips. "What are you doing?"

"Just like those stupid adventure films." He grinned, affecting a long, bristling growl. "I'll hold them off, sweetheart. Very noble, don't you think?" His expression sobered. "She's a geomancer, Ava Sandrino. What else will slow her down but another geomancer?"

"No." Beside her, Ava felt Sariel shift. "They will denature you. At the bone-fires—the hide-behind told me what that means."

"I'll get out of it. I always do." He gave the handgun a smart tap. "That kid won't. If the Guild does not claim him, the Emperor Tong will fill his skull with lead."

"Fifteen seconds, Lake," said the woman on the ridge.

"But his father—"

"Listen." Oliver bent until their foreheads touched. She saw the varnish of freckles on his cheeks. "It will be all right, Sandrino. Inday will declare herself. They will arrest her and put the boy in quarantine, but you and the wraith do not have to give the gatekeeper your names. Ask for Harriette Melgar. She is an interworld barrister. Tell her about the child, and tell her that Absalom Lake's brother sent you." He glanced over her head. "There are guild hospitals at every stop along the way. If your wraith has not healed up by then, you can request that he be seen at one."

Upon the ridge, the rifle roared. "Time's up," the woman said. She descended on a torrent of shale, landing in the crosshairs of the gliding searchlights. *Seknat*, thought Ava. *They called her Seknat*. She was straight-backed and tawny, her dusky eyes ablaze beneath an iron helmet. Behind her, the strand of shadows followed.

"You heard the lady." Oliver knelt. "Shoot with both eyes open. There will be knights in the field. Oh, and Ava—" he flicked the switchblade open, plunging it into the frozen earth. "Don't speak to the river ghosts. They like gossip, treasure, and dead sailors."

A patchwork of lines fell from the blade. They chased each other across the soil in gossamer rings. When he gestured, the weapon shook. Hazy ichor rose, spun into squalls by an eastern gale. Ava smelled rain and rot, and the bite of the hangman's sap as it oozed from the veins of trees. The poison storm broke, blistered by starlight and sparks. The row of knights ground to a jumbled halt.

Only Seknat advanced. She let the rifle fall, spots of gold blooming where she went. Her image shimmered and danced.

"You're still here, Ava," said Oliver, hoarsely. "Get out, now!"

Dimly, Ava realized that she had lost his pocket square. "Lake," she said, face streaming in the flux of the cutting draft. "The Guild—we can't leave you—"

Seknat cleared the crossroads, armored hand outstretched. She snapped her fingers. The switchblade came loose, pulling up clumps of petrified tubers and roots. It quivered in midair.

"So, this is what the Eighth Pike does to geomancers." She perched on a bank of sea glass and cockleshells. With a flick of her wrist, the knife began to swivel. "Only children need objects to harness the earth lines. Your handler has gelded you." Her helmet tilted. A white vulture glared upon its beaten crest. "I can get you an audience, you know. The black-market cities are freedom beyond compare." The knife wobbled. Its point inched towards Oliver. "There are no rules where I come from," she said. "No fat senators bickering about policy. They use you like a racehorse. They will shoot you like one, too, when the cocaine rots your mind, or when age takes your legs. Haven't you had enough?"

"I'll tell you when I've had enough." Oliver spat through his teeth. Behind them, the wind changed course. The bleached circles under his knees turned to strings of ash, binding his legs to the plates of bedrock below.

"Oliver, stop." Ava lurched forward, arms outstretched. She hardly felt it when Sariel caught her by the waist. "We should talk. The black-market cities might give us asylum—all of us."

"Seknat is a liar." Oliver raised his head, lips peeling and pale. "The black-market cities are the pisspot of the One O'clock King. The Pit Lords are just as likely to sell the boy to a brothel as they are to feed him. Your masters search only for profit and turncoats, and I will give them neither." He tried to stand, but the cords of ash held fast. "They're waiting, Ava. That boat won't move without you."

The wind soughed. Voices murmured at the guardhouse gate, dull behind a curtain of hangman's sap. Seknat shrugged. "Too bad," she said. Her fingers clicked again.

The switchblade sang as it sheared the air. Oliver gave a ragged shout. He twisted, pulling hard against his filmy bonds. They scattered and broke, sliding like tentacles into the bowl of the earth. He sprang to his feet. The knife clipped his ear, embedding itself in the post of a burned-out lamp. "Run," he said.

The geomancers met in a clash of molten light. Ava screamed. Her nails left crescents in Sariel's arm. She tried in vain to winnow one from the other, but they moved with a speed that she could not follow, bodies draining into shrouds of blinding sunspots.

Like candle flames eating through parchment, a black hole opened in the snow. Oliver and Seknat came apart and collided. Against the limb-stealing cold that poured from the void, Ava caught a glimpse of his bloodied mouth and the shattered glass of his wristwatch. Then, the darkness closed. The universe shut its door, and they were gone.

Heart pounding, she bolted to where flecks of soot hung on the air, covering her face against the hangman's sap while she paced the upturned ground. "Go," she said to Sariel. "The fortune-teller and her son are aboard that boat. If I don't show, they will find the sunrise barge and run for Tesalonica, like you planned."

"Ava." Sariel spoke her name, soft and terse. "They are not coming back."

"What do you mean?" Her fingers had knotted themselves together. Her toes left imprints on the charred earth. *Chasms and ravines in the black market cities*, she thought. *They will pull the magic from his spine. He will never be found.*

"They are geomancers. They take their brawls up north, into the shelves between worlds. They would level cities if they did not. Time passes differently there. If they do resurface, it will have been the blink of an eye for them, and nearly a month for us." She turned to face him. He was standing properly, bearing his weight on the broken limb like it was whole. "This smokescreen will not last forever," he said. "And the slipstreams close in one hour."

"Is he alive?" The words left dents in her

heart. "You're a wraith. You can feel every drop along the earth-lines."

"I cannot tell. They move faster than a human should. Besides, a wraith is no geomancer who can send his soul flying throughout all the worlds. We put down roots. I can see only to the shore of the Landless Kingdoms." He hesitated. "If he lives, you cannot help him here. Not in manacles, behind the walls of a prison." He held out his hands, and she felt the draw of the tether between them. "I can search for him when they have settled. Please."

Ava shuddered. She took a short step towards him, then another, and another. Sariel began a stilted run down a hill studded with deep-sea dwellers relinquished by ancient tides. She followed, flinching at the volley of gunfire that boomed above. Her eyes found the foam of lamp-lit waves.

In the white poppy fields, winter thistles left burrs in the pleats of her skirt. They smelled like antiseptic from a backstreet apothecary. Between breaths, she felt Sariel, bright and warm as a meteor at landfall. He was right, she thought, over the beating of her pulse. There would be no help for Oliver if she found herself on the wrong side of a prison door.

The meadow went by in fits and starts. She pictured Inday, holding fast to Caleb on the loveseat. The light of the moon and the weight of her death streamed from her in sacred pools.

*You will have to start again*, the hide-behind crooned. *What was it for?*

For Demetra, perhaps, who gathered her banknotes and traded them for silence and silks.

Up ahead, a frigatebird trilled. Starting again did not seem so bad. Wealth was everywhere, and she was tired of spending it alone, half-asleep on the velvet couch with a cobwebbed radio and stale notions of the Orchid Coast.

The ground dipped beneath her. Her chest was a thirsty forge. Up ahead, Sariel vaulted over a stand of pink driftwood. When she scrambled past the white horns of timber, something seized her by the coat and tugged. The rattle of grass filled her ears. She went down amongst the snow and waxen flowers.

Ava rolled over. Her heart sank at the sight of Red, leaping into the beam of the lighthouse. The war wraith was a rawboned streak against the stars and city lights.

"Sariel!" Ava twisted onto her belly and stood, tilting towards the driftwood stand. "Look out!"

Against the glowing sea, she saw him slow.

Red pounced. They fell together in a snarl of limbs and horns. The luster of a torch and the creak of leather flooded the space behind them.

Something inside of Ava went still and cold. She raised her arms, clasping her hands behind her head before Captain Shaw had the chance to say, "Stop! The House of Tong commands you."

"Good evening, Ezra." Steel licked her nape where he rested the muzzle of his gun. "You couldn't wait for the warrants, could you? They'll arrest you if they find out what you've done. His Holiness doesn't traffic with black market hounds."

"I knew you would run," he said, winded and thick. "Your geomancer is gone. What were you going to do, Ava? Search for the Northern Dark alone, or sail for Tesalonica? You would not last an hour. They make our swindlers look like saints." Along the eastern slope, knights in green converged, glowing with aether and iron. Sharply, he whistled for Red. "Bring him here."

Red dragged Sariel to his knees by the horns and wrestled him into the halo of the plastic torch. The four of them stood, covered in yellow poppy dust. Ezra threw down his light and ground the revolver into her neck. "Look," he said, voice fractured with anger. "Look at him—

does that look like a man to you?"

"He knows when he was born." Snowflakes settled on her eyelashes. They turned to water when she blinked. "He knows where he comes from, and he knows where he is going. That's all. Shouldn't that be all?"

"Ava." The back of his hand struck her head. "Is your Paper House money not enough? You had to help yourself to rare books and pianos from Babel. What a sickness to have!"

"Your mother is swimming in rare books and pianos," said Ava. "Your father very nearly owns a bank. You never had a word to say about that."

"They are not knights." His glove squeaked against the weapon's grip.

"Neither am I." She laughed, low and loud. "You are always so certain. I suppose that's what I liked about you."

From the lee of the field, the others arrived. They clattered through the windblown stems, trailing pollen and lamplight. "Wait," said Captain Shaw. He waved, halting their approach. She turned to face him, and was unsurprised to find the revolver dangling, forgotten, from his hand.

"I never changed, Ezra." Her words were soft, a riddle that ached between them. "You know what I am: fancy wines and trips to the coast.

You saw it the moment you laid eyes on me."

He drew close. The mail beneath his tabard rang. For a moment, she was a girl once more, listening to his ramblings about the Eastern Church and its railway dreams.

"I can help you, Ava," he said. "This city is a hard place, especially for Orchid Coast girls. You came from famine. I don't think you ever got right." He holstered the gun. "Maybe you weren't meant for the barracks, but this Paper House business is bad. I can fix this. We can make this go away."

"And the wraith?" Sweat beaded her lips. "Can you make that go away, too?"

There was a terrible pause. She tensed, waiting for the cuff of his fist. "Are you mad?" He crimsoned. "I offered you decent work, and you would not leave the brothels. Now, you're running off on the heels of a brimstone beast!"

Slowly, the color left his cheeks, fading over the birthmark that looked like a scar. "Ezra," she said. "I did not mean to make you angry."

She had spoken the words hundreds of times, running her hands across the blemish on his face. Its raspberry stain was the first thing that she noticed at Agia Marina, stepping off an Orchid Coast ship and onto the platform where he stood in the cruel heat. He bowed and took her checkered suitcase. "They sent me to fetch you," he said. His dogtooth was missing, knocked out in a fight. "Welcome to New Dera."

He was two years older, and reminded her often. Their first kiss tasted like coffee and khat, alone in the cellars on Deliverance Eve. "I wanted to be a mariner," he told her, while her fingers lined up stamps that would guide her letters home. "No one respects a sailor, though. All they get is salty bread and whores."

Ava tried to summon some tenderness, a flicker of love or want. Her memories of him were unpaired jigsaw bits: the scrape of concrete against her shins, the thrill of his prick in her mouth, kneeling in the window of the highest tower. Afterwards, he took the makeshift oud from her hands and dragged his fingers over its strings, mesmerized and bemused. He only gave to beggars when it was a spectacle on holy days. He brawled with stable hands and foreign squires, and his face grew thunderous when their proctor praised her aim.

Behind her, Red stirred. Ava's mind raced. If he had the good sense to run, she could buy Sariel at least five minutes. Inday and Caleb would find the sunrise barge and land in Tesalonica with a wraith to guard them. If he did not, they were both dead, and the soothsayer would be a woman alone in a country without rules.

Ava dashed water from her nose and chin. Her last remembrance of Ezra took flight, quick as a cloudburst in spring. "You were right, Captain," she said. "No one respects a sailor. They bow to officers with thankful ladies on their arms."

He stared at her, speechless in the wake of his wrath. The metal of the handgun had warmed against her breasts. Its hammer clicked under her thumb. She tugged it from the pocket inside her coat, put the barrel between his eyes and pulled the trigger.

Ezra Shaw made no sound as he fell. Ava saw Red push Sariel facedown into the dirt. The war wraith flew at her, leaving her flat on her back, pinioned between the metal greaves. Strong fingers crushed her throat.

In the gloaming, a knight cried out. "The Captain is shot," he said. "Not too close—Red's got her. Bring the chains and stock prod!"

The snowfall and darkness were nearly opaque. Her vision dimmed; she drooled into the sandy ground, wrenching her head towards the glimmer of water. "Careful," someone hollered. "I said—careful—he's coming this way—"

Sariel crashed into Red. The hand around her throat grew slack. Ava gasped, taking in the icy air. The two wraiths rolled over and over, coming to rest between the roots of a barren hawthorn. In a flash of sinew and skin, Sariel tore himself loose.

"Run," said Ava as he scrambled to his feet. "You have to run."

Beyond the skeletal tree, the knights had gathered. They took the slope, slow and skittish, the chime of manacles tinny between them. Sariel watched Red, shoulders heaving. The metal collar showed a dim polish around her corded neck.

"Listen." Blood from a skinned knee soaked her dress. "They are going to put you back in that birdcage and send you to the alchemist in Selang. You need to go."

He glanced at her. She saw the briefest flicker of scarlet. Then, he turned to Red. A silence stretched between them, vacant and porcelain.

"Sister," he said, as the circle of lamplight closed in. "What is your name?"

Red spoke. Her words came quickly, in a soft spate of Khardsog and French. Head tilted, she peered at Sariel. "You know my name," she replied.

"It is what they have called you." Sariel put out his hands like a priest after alms. The night seemed to change, gathering in ripples and folds around him. "What did we call you, sister, on the fever ships? On the banks of the Landless Kingdoms?"

Her green eyes flashed. "Malazin," she said. "That is my fever ship name."

In the surging blizzard, Ava kept still. *They can compel each other*, Oliver had said. *If they are strong enough.* The thought filled her with a heavy, nameless dread.

She did not move when the lamplight engulfed her, or when she was seized by a knight wearing steel gloves. A strange current passed between Sariel and Malazin. It spilled from the taproots of the distant meridian, entering the bowels of ships and exiting through labyrinths of markets and mines that swallowed wraiths. Malazin was bound by invisible ropes. Her body swayed with the movement of Sariel's head.

"Aether bullets," somebody said. "Bring them, fast!"

Against the blustering waves, the war wraith spun. She charged, ripping the knight from Ava in a single motion. There was a symphony of splitting fabric and crunching bone. Bent at the waist, a pool of blood and the wreckage of a man beneath her, Malazin glared through the snow.

"Go," she said. "It is not every day that a wraith gets free."

Ava bolted for the hawthorn tree, falling and rising and clawing through soil until she reached its withered arms. Sariel took her shaking hand. Together, they stumbled shoreward, away from the poppy field and down the rocky curve of an empty hill.

"The bullets," someone screamed. "Hurry! There's something wrong with this one—"

Ahead, the ocean flattened into a shining disk. They lost sight of the boats that drifted in the deeper waters. When the hill turned into a yellow road, the sound of gunfire shattered and ebbed.

Sariel stopped. Stones flew beneath his toes. He looked up at where the meadow was buried in clouds.

"Malazin." Ava shook him by the shoulder. The name slid, knife-sharp, along her tongue. "You did something to her." The heat that rose from him coaxed pins and needles into her hand. "That night at my flat, did you do the same to me?"

He stared at her. Shards of moonlight filled the wells of his eyes. "I did nothing to you," he said. "You are a human. A wraith can persuade you only with words." The lines of his face tightened, and she saw the leavings of shame and fear. "In the brimstone mines and the alchemist's quarters, I was forced in everything I did. I would not wish that for anyone."

Ava glanced up at the meadow. She knew it would be minutes before the knights regrouped, but she could not help herself. "You gave her to them," she said. "You put your orders in her brain, and now she is dead."

"She was going to kill you." He made a pleading gesture. "I have never done it before. I will never do it again."

She reached through the tempest, touching his chest with rime-hardened fingers. "You are right. I do not know you." Her words were fletched and barbed, but they flew wide, landing somewhere else and with a gentleness she did not intend. "We are strangers, Sariel. I suppose that most of us is worn out. That's something, at least. It's a long way to go on ships and trains that we did not buy tickets for."

Shouted commands tumbled down with the wind. Sariel held her palm against him until its veins stuttered to life. "You still think of coming with me," he said. "I will follow the trail of our river ghosts, but they do not know me, and I do not know them. They are just as likely to drown me as they are to show me the way."

Madame Rummage and her warnings about black market brimstone and river ghosts turned to sand in her mouth. She was filled with things that had no words: bright triptychs of the Orchid Coast, the handgun she had dropped along the way, the weight of a child in her belly.

"There are exits in the slipstream," he said when she did not reply. "There are places in the southern oceans. You could be comfortable there. If I am wrong, the tracking metals will burn beyond the Northern Dark. It would not do for you to be found with me."

Below them, a teal schooner bobbed in the harbor where the fortune-teller and her son waited. Ava did not need to look at it to know that its sails were folded against the mast, ready for the bone-white blast of the slipstream, or that its prow was painted with the beak and wings of a blue ibis.

She closed her eyes and saw Oliver Lake, vanishing into a wound in the world. The thought of becoming someone else in the salt spray of a distant island, away from Sariel and his unknown fate, left her empty and weightless.

Tendrils of warmth crept up her arm. "Our city is dull, my dear." She smiled. "Nine years, and it has given me everything it can. I am curious about Blackwater and this One O'clock King."

Far away, the lamps ignited.

"Ava," said Sariel, and nothing more. They followed each other to the foot of the black pier, where the train tracks lay dead, and old wood crumbled at the touch of barnacles and salt.

Made in the USA
Monee, IL
09 November 2019